The Making of an Assassin

Henry J. Howley

To Father O'connor

A wonderful man.

Harry Howley.

Dart Publications

Copyright © 1992: Henry J. Howley
All rights reserved; no part of this publication may be reproduced, stored in a retrieval system or transmitted, in any form or by any means, electronic, mechanical, photocopying, recording or otherwise, without prior written permission of Henry J. Howley.

Manufactured in the United States of America

Library of Congress Number: 92-071924

ISBN 0-9633061-0-3

Cover Design: Art Duperault

Dart Publications
329 LaRosas
Venice, FL 32487
1-813-426-2422

Many Thanks to my wife, Sylvia, my son David, and my daughter, Susan, for their help and encouragement while I wrote this book. My old school friends are not to be forgotten either.

Henry J. Howley
1992

Chapter 1

The rain was falling lightly, as it had been since early evening. It was a warm rain this August night in 1980.

Heedless, Brian Tilson sat on the curb with his head in his hands. The fact that he was soaking wet seemed not to matter to him. In the last three weeks it seemed that everything that could go wrong, had.

Brian's thoughts went back to the day three weeks ago when his boss, Mr. Crawford, had fallen and broken his ankle.

Brian had worked for Mr. Crawford for the past eighteen months doing household repairs, roofing and siding, and he was also taking courses twice a week in electric wiring and installation. Brian liked the work and he enjoyed working with Mr. Crawford and was trying to learn as much as he could to make up for his poor start.

He had always had the urge to better himself and at first had worked for Jack Ellis as an apprentice electrician. He was to start full time as soon as he left school, but, three days before he left, he had come down with appendicitis. With the complications that ensued he was in the hospital for eight weeks. Jack could not hold the job open for him, and he lost his chance.

Now, since his boss had fallen, he was out of luck and work again. He had been informed by Mr. Crawford that it would be at least three months before he could get back on the job. Brian didn't like that one bit. He hated to be idle. And, he needed the money.

On top of that, the day after the accident, he arrived home to find that his sister Annie, who was six years older than he, was home again to live. He tried to understand and wasn't one to complain. He loved his sister and her boy, and he got along well with her husband, Bill. When Annie had married and moved out, he had sorely missed her. So, he had mixed feelings about what he really hoped would be a temporary situation.

On Saturday afternoon, Brian and his steady girlfriend, Brenda Watson, went over to Renee Rowe's wedding. In the evening they all went round to Renee's brother John's house for a few drinks and games. After they had been drinking for a while, Brian got Terri Rowe in a bedroom and was kissing her up a storm when Brenda barged into the room and turned on the light. There was an unholy row and he'd been thrown out of the house. Brenda went home with Donny Clay. Brian knew that Clay had been casting sheep eyes at Brenda for quite some time. Donny had a good job as an apprentice plumber and played football as a semi-pro.

Donny was a big feller, over six feet and about one hundred and ninety pounds. That was way over Brian's five-feet-eight and one hundred and forty-five pounds. Donny didn't care how much he hurt a feller either. Brian thought it better to leave well alone. He sighed deeply.

The front door was locked, as usual, when he got home. Brian reached through the letterbox and got a hold of the string which held the key. When he pulled it, no key was attached. He cursed Annie and started around the street to the back door. It, too, was locked. Finding the scullery window open just a crack, he shinnied up the waste pipe, stood on the window sill, and reached into the window. He had to force his arm up through the opening, but managed to release the catch. It had been three years since he done this old trick. He had put on size and weight since then, and he found himself blowing from the exertion. Finally, he made it and slithered through the window hoping none of the nosy neighbours had seen him.

Brian stood on the draining board by the sink and then jumped to the floor, squelching across it in his sodden shoes before deciding to take them off.

Hanging his soaking clothes in the hallway, he made his way up to his attic bedroom. He was in a terrible, depressed state of mind.

After breakfast the next morning, he decided to ride round to Brenda's on his bike since she only lived a few streets away at Cross Flats Street.

Brenda wasn't at all happy to see him.

"What the 'ell do you want round 'ere? You bare-faced

bugger, after last night I'm Donny's girl now. So, shove off, ya bloody nut. 'Appen I'll tell him that ya been round. 'E may want to push your face in."

She'd rambled on almost all in one breath. Brian was devastated. In a matter of three short weeks his whole world had fallen apart. He didn't know what was best to do.

All week long he tramped the streets looking for work. By the following Sunday he was getting desperate. By Monday morning he knew he had to start doing something, so he decided to go down to the Job Center on Park Avenue to see if they could fix him up with a job. He was willing to try almost anything. But they informed him they didn't have a thing to offer. Now he felt worse than ever.

As he turned away from the counter, his eye was drawn to an army recruitment poster. "Why not?" he thought and jotted down the address.

At the Recruitment Center he filled out some forms and was given some booklets describing all the wonderful benefits of army life. He decided to talk it over with his dad.

Later after dinner, he brought up the subject with his mother and father. "Dad, ah 'ave been thinking of joining t'army," he said. "There is no work round 'ere that's any good, and ah don't want to be a drag on you and Mam. Ah talked it over with t'army sergeant and 'e assures me that ah can continue me schooling for to be an electrician, and when ah complete the course, ah will get extra stripes and money. With army trade grades ah can get a job anywhere after ah finish me time. With the grades ah already 'ave ah can even go for more education. There is a chance of officers' school. There will be travel and ah can look for a better place to live than this crummy 'ole of Leeds." He paused. "It's either that or Australia."

Mr. Tilson looked at his son. "Don't take everything wot that sergeant says as gospel. Ya could get sent to Northern Ireland where those mad Irish Catholic bastards are killing each other. Those Popists 'ate us Protestants with a passion. They're crazy drunken pigs as ya know. They come over 'ere and steal our jobs and work cheap and ruin everything. But maybe ya can 'elp change things."

Brian filled out the papers. After two weeks he was called for an examination and passed with flying colors. The following week he was called to report to a training camp. He thought to himself, "Ah'm going to get into that electric school and make the best soldier that ever was." He was looking forward to a brand-new experience and bettering himself.

Brian reported to Strenton Camp to join the Blue Jackets, a crack infantry battalion. The next sixteen weeks were the toughest of his young life, but he was determined to make good and keep out of trouble.

Chapter 2

Another recruit at the camp, was Bob Day, a young coal miner from Batley in Yorkshire. He was sturdily built, with shoulders like an ox. He was five-feet-ten, weighed one hundred and eighty pounds and had blue eyes and jet black hair. He was always ready with a bit of repartee—a nice and easy-going young fellow. Bob hated the coal mines and the dirt, and was also looking to better himself. He and Brian became good friends. Bob wanted to travel and chose the army to pay for his traveling. All the recruits had a lot to learn.

Basic training finally ended. Now the men were at a camp for riot training high on the moors.

For the first time in his life Brian came up against harsh reality. He had been brought up in a nice, decent, normal, working-class home with a good and caring mother. His father tried to do his best for the family, and his older sister showed him love and affection, sharing his everyday cares and worries.

Brian had been an average student in school, and although his folks hadn't been regular church-going people, he'd attended bible classes with his friends. But he didn't go regularly as he was ashamed of his patched clothes and worn shoes. He missed out on a lot of things that normal kids did—movies and things like that. His father had never held a good paying job; money was hard to come by and the family had some rough times. Wet shoes were just one of the things he had to put up with—that and threadbare clothes. Going to bed hungry was normal.

What made it worse was the knowledge that his mother often went without things for herself to feed him and his sister. She patched and repatched and struggled to keep things going.

Mrs. Tilson always tried to help her children with their studies. She realized that Brian would speak the Yorkshire dialect when he was out with the boys and at school, but she spent long hours teaching her children how to speak properly as best she could. So Brian quite naturally would speak dialect to his dad and other men, then almost no dialect when he spoke to his sister or mother.

Very early on he realized that he was being raised in a class society, that there was a big difference between rich and poor. While reading the newspapers at the public library, he didn't take long to find out that there often seemed to be one law for the rich and another for the poor. Monied people had all the privileges. It was something he never forgot.

As all little children, he dreamed of the day he could and would make it big.

He'd played on the football team with the school and they'd played rough, too. He was smaller than many of the fellows and lost more battles than he had won. His opponents, however, sure knew they had been in a fight. Brian was not easily subdued.

But this was different. He was being trained, not just being shown, but trained how to inflict bodily harm and pain on others. People he had never seen. Regardless of race, color, male or female, Catholic or Protestant, young or old. It turned his stomach. He didn't like it and his soul rebelled against it.

He had never dreamed that something as wrong as this even existed.

Brian read that a world war had been fought to stop atrocities like this. His sergeant, Sergeant Jim Buckley, frequently berated him for not beating hard enough on the practice dummies. "Now Tilson," he would yell, 'ow is the stomach today? Come on, ya little twat, ah'll make a man of ya yet, in spite of everything. If ya broke ya'r mother's 'eart ya won't break mine. Take that there truncheon and beat on that dummy—if it was an IRA, man would ya be so careful? Come on, 'it it, 'it it, 'it it!"

He would glare at Brian. "Face front when ah tell ya, ya squint-eyed pillack." He seemed to put more pressure on Brian than the others.

One day the entire squad was marched to the back of a long abandoned building and told to dig a trench. Then the men were ordered down in the trench.

The men stayed in the hole with ponchos for cover for a full 14 days. On the second day, Lieutenant Ragwood came to make an inspection. Casually, he unzipped his fly, urinated on the heads of the hapless young men. Sergeant Buckley followed his example, spraying it all around so, as he said, "Ya all get ya'r fair share." One of the seventeen-year-olds came charging out of the trench, rushing for the lieutenant, and was tackled and frog-marched away to detention for a week. The boys were stunned. This was unbelievable and couldn't be happening!

"Toughen the blighters up, don't you know," said the officer. "Makes men out of boys."

The recruits ate and slept out their time in the trench. At the end, tired and smelly, they marched back to their barracks.

Much sadder and wiser, they were disillusioned by the ignominy of their harsh treatment at the hands of their own officers, who they felt should have known better.

When they got back to their barracks, the first news they heard was that the officer had been dismissed from the service and Sergeant Buckley had been severely reprimanded. This meant nothing, since the same barbaric practices were still going on, only hidden better.

But as one small soldier said, "If this is being a man, to 'ell with it!"

Chapter 3

After another sixteen weeks of riot and toughening-up training, Brian and Bob were told to pack their gear. They were ordered right away as replacements to Northern Ireland.

As Brian boarded the truck that was about to take him to the airport, he didn't feel happy. He was apprehensive and afraid. This was yet again a new experience. Neither boy had flown before, and they both had just a little fear of the unknown. They had hoped they would not be sent to Northern Ireland. Having been brought up with children who had relatives there, they felt it might be difficult to enforce the law.

They decided it would be best to conduct themselves like the men and soldiers they had been trained to be. They were going to a new country. It was an adventure, so they tried to cover their fear and act very grown-up.

When the plane landed at Belfast Airport, they cleared the stream of traffic, collected their baggage, then went out and had a cup of tea. For the last ten hours they had been too excited to eat. Now they were beginning to feel really hungry.

"Ah hope the perishing army 'asn't forgotten abart us," said Brian.

"Aye," replied Bob, "that would be something 'eh?"

The airport emptied and there they stood, two scrawny seventeen-year-old kids in ill-fitting khaki uniforms. They stood out like sore thumbs.

Not knowing what to do next, they simply stood and waited. Finally a big black car without any markings on it pulled up with a screech of brakes. Out jumped a large man in a blue suit.

"All right," he snarled, "get in the car and make it quick."

The boys threw their gear in back and followed it as fast as they could as the car pulled away from the curb.

Brian nudged Bob in the ribs as he looked down. "Oh my God!," he croaked, and pointed down to the guns laid on the floor of the car under the seats. "We 'ave been kidnapped by the IRA." Beads of sweat stood out on his forehead.

False alarm. They had been lucky. The men detailed to pick them up had been delayed and their late arrival made them rush the boys off without any explanation. They were delivered safely to their barracks. They had some anxious moments first and a scare for their introduction to Northern Ireland.

Sergeant Polis, Brian's new sergeant, had been raised in the Old Elephant and Castle district in London—one of the toughest places on earth. As he grew older, he became more aggressive and finally ended up in the dock on serious wounding charges.

As often as not, the magistrates solved local problems and at the same time helped the recruiting drive by giving miscreants the option of going to jail or joining the army.

Army life suited Polis. The rough and tumble, regular food and exercise had soon made a good physical specimen of him. He made a success of army life, but he had a mean, cruel streak. He was a product of his heredity, upbringing and environment. As he progressed and earned himself a stripe, he took his spite and meanness out on the young soldiers under him. This was army life. It didn't bother the officers. They likened what they saw to toughness. He'd made sergeant a few times and had been busted back by the time troubles broke out in Northern Ireland.

Polis was the ideal type of man the English authorities wanted in charge to try to control the unruly people of the region.

He was the only Southerner in the company. All the rest were Northerners, Yorkshire and Lancasterhire men. He enjoyed himself from the first day, ordering people around. He made them wait until he made up his mind as to when they could go about their business. It gave him a feeling of power which he reveled in.

This, then, was one of the men who took control of Brian and the other young impressionable men. No more than boys who were molded by these brutes for the next three years. Mold them they did in their own savage images.

Sergeant Polis's idea of control was to use as much force as possible—brute force. He didn't agree with the idea of trying to talk to the people. His idea was to subdue them as soon as possible. He thought, and rightly so, that this was how the British Empire was formed in the first place. The people of his sector soon recognized this and cleared away as soon as they saw his squad approach.

This was soon noticed by the army observers and duly reported to the higher echelon. Polis' methods quickly became army policy. The people who advocated a slower, milder approach to the problem were shouldered aside when the reports came in that these rougher tactics were proving to be right. What they didn't take into account was that the people had never seen anything like this before. They didn't know how to react. After awhile they adjusted and planned retaliation. They began to meet brute force and brutality with like force, only more so. The situation soon went from bad to worse.

When Brian and his buddy came to Belfast, the conditions were as bad as could be. Neither side would admit it was in the wrong. Neither side would even talk to the other. The soldiers had been welcomed at first, but with men like Sergeant Polis, they didn't hold their popularity for long and the stones began to fly their way.

As events became worse, the patrols intensified. It wasn't long before casualties mounted. The army constantly replaced men and materials. For various reasons (mental adjustments and injuries) men were sent back to England almost daily without notice. The young men of the region began to throw fire bombs (bottles filled with gas and oil) and to plant explosives in cars and set them off by remote control.

Chapter 4

During the summer months the squad did a daily routine check of shopper's parcels; as the new guys, they had taken this routine duty over from another company.

A report came in that on College Square at East and Davis Street, explosives were being carried in shopping bags.

Brian approached a good-looking girl about twenty-years-old.

As she came up to the barricade, he smiled at her and motioned to her to open the bag she carried. She stepped up close to him, and as she did so, he slung his gun over his shoulder. She came up real quick with her knee, right into his groin. He looked at her with a deeply shocked and pained expression then slumped to the ground retching his stomach up. This was the first time he'd been caught like that. The pain made him sick as a dog. The girl just walked away as though nothing had happened. She never said a word, in fact, she didn't even cast a backward glance.

Later, on the Croyne Road he had another bad experience. A fight developed between two gangs of youths. Bricks and stones were flying all over the place. A stone bounded on the road and struck Brian's right knee, raising a large bruise that was sore for days.

The next morning, the knee was very stiff, and the boys told him to report sick. He hobbled across to sick bay. The doctor took one look at him and almost threw him out the door, telling him not to come back unless he had something really wrong with him.

"What the 'ell does 'e think this is?" Brian thought out loud. He painfully made his way back to the barracks. There the rest of the company was waiting for him, with a pair of crutches and a wheelchair.

"You poor old kid, did ya 'urt your little knee then? Come let us kiss it better," they teased. Brian knew then that he had been had.

The firebombs were the worst. They could only try to dodge them and beat them out when they struck. One day Brian didn't dodge quickly enough and the petrol and oil mixture spilt onto his boots causing him to do a war dance, stamping and beating out the flames. He was plenty scared. All the other guys could do was whistle a dance tune and clap their hands. When they returned to the barracks later and he took off his boots, he found half a dozen good sized blisters on his ankles and feet.

As the other men said, "Ah' rub some vaseline on it. It could have been worse. It could 'a been your dick, old man, and then what would you 'ave done?"

These sorts of things went on all the time with no let up. The only difference was that some days were worse than others: the nervous strain of never knowing what might happen, and the grapevine news that some poor bugger in another company had got his, or someone had been disabled.

When Brian first talked to the recruiting officer, he'd been asked to outline his education and work skills. He'd been told that further training would be available for various skills like his. He had asked about electrical work and had been told that with his experience and four O and four A school levels he would be considered for further education.

Brian approached his officer, Captain Stables, and asked about the possibilities of further education. The captain was incredulous and told him, "Gad, man, don't you think I have enough trouble keeping you chappies alive without you bothering me with your silly efforts at education? Come see me in six months, that is if you are still alive. We live from day to day, don't you know? Now, bugger off."

Brian was slow to anger, but he didn't like the answer. It rankled. He wrote to his member of Parliament for Leeds, trying to explain his position and asking for an explanation. All he got was a scathing letter in reply, telling him everyone had to do his duty.

Lying on his bunk with his mind in turmoil, he reached for the letter he received from his M.P. and went over it again. As he did so, he realized that he had been lied to, that all the promises that the recruiting sergeant made, were just that, promises. He was no better off than he had been in Leeds. In fact, he was worse off. All he could look forward to was the same dirty, dangerous days that he was now enduring and nothing at the end of them.

The bile rose in his throat.

So, he went out with the boys, got good and drunk, and ended up in the guard house. He never brought up the subject of education again, but it hardened his resolve. Somebody was going to pay for deceiving him and pay they did. But not the ones who did it. More's the pity.

The men were rousted out of a sound sleep in the wee hours of the morning and ordered into the Land Rovers. "Move as fast as possible," they were told. They'd had word from a local Carey (an informer) that a noted and badly wanted IRA man was sleeping at a house at Pendleton Walk in the New Lodge area. There was no time to eat. They rushed out. This was not unusual. Brian was the driver on this foray, so didn't take part in any of the action. He had to stay with the truck and keep the engine running, ready to move when ordered.

It was still dark and overcast when they reached the street to be cordoned off. Four vehicles, with six men in each, comprised the detail. The men took up their positions and the search began. But there was strong opposition immediately. Firing began and casualties were taken.

This was the first time Brian had seen flowing blood. Jim Hughes, one of the men in his squad, came staggering back to the truck, and Brian assisted him into the back. When he looked down, Brian saw Jim's pants covered with blood. Jim was hit bad.

Brian no sooner had gotten him settled in the back, with Harry Lockwood (the medic) attending to him, then George Walker was carried up. He was also in a bad way. Brian was ordered to take him to the Queen Victoria Military Section of the hospital right away.

George Walker never returned to the unit. He was "invalided" out of the army. He was a big loss. Walker had a very good tenor voice and lifted the spirits of the men many times when things were going badly. He was always ready to give a cheerful tune when needed.

When Brian returned to the scene of the action, everything

was quiet, everything had been cleaned up. The search had turned up nothing. In a matter of three hours, it was all over and no one had been arrested. Another case of over-reaction.

The small streets were like rabbit warrens. The locals could be fighting one minute and the next minute could be miles away. It was all terribly frustrating.

Chapter 5

Four weeks passed and Brian was getting used to Belfast and finding his way around pretty well. He and Bob had gone into a shop to buy sweets. When they came out, they saw a young lady pulling at the rear wheel of her bicycle. The wheel was loose, so Brian, being a gentleman, walked over to her.

"Something wrong?" he inquired. "You seem to be in trouble."

"The wheel 'as come loose and I don't know how to fix it," she answered.

Brian smiled at her and bent down to check the fastening. The wing nut holding the wheel had worked loose. He flipped the bike over, straightened the wheel, and tightened the nuts on both sides, then he checked the other wheel to make sure they were both all right. He flipped the bike back over on its wheels and presented it to the girl.

"There you are, me dear, as good as new," he said.

She thanked him, mounted the bike and rode away.

Three days later, while on patrol in the Prestwick Park area, Brian saw the girl hanging out clothes at Number 25, Sloan Street. She smiled at him and called out, "Thank you, again." The next day he saw her near the school. She smiled and this was Brian's cue to stop and talk for a few minutes.

Saturday found Bob and Brian at St. Monica's Church Hall for a dance. There was the girl, serving cake, so it wasn't long before he went over and spoke to her.

"Will ya dance wi' me?" he asked.

"I'll be free in about ten minutes. I work one hour in rotation with the other girls. As soon as I'm relieved, I will be able to dance," she replied.

When Brian saw another girl take over the cake stall, he

returned and again asked her for their dance. When the dance ended, he took her over to Bob and they introduced themselves formally.

Her name was Maureen Foley. He told her he already knew where she lived. She had two brothers, no sisters, and her brother Bill was still living at home; he was a heavy-weight boxer and was doing real well. He had a little car and was thinking of buying a pub, Maureen told the boys.

When the dance finished, Brian walked Maureen home. On the way back to the barracks, he had to be careful. He wasn't supposed to be out alone and could have gotten into trouble if the sergeant found out.

Brian made a date with Maureen and they were to meet again. He couldn't get her out of his mind. She was eighteen years old, her hair was raven black, and she was about five-foot-six. He guessed she weighed about eight stone and he knew she had a lovely figure. She was really bright and lots of fun to be with.

Bob, of course, spread the news that Brian had clicked and he had to take a lot of good-natured ribbing from the rest of the squad, especially from Sergeant Polis, who never missed the chance to needle him.

For the next few weeks, things went along easily. The nights were long, cold and wet. The patrols were not easy, but he saw Maureen as much as he could—always in the evening. He never seemed to be off duty on weekends and since she worked part time, it wasn't easy. They went to the movies or took a walk, and he had to be content with that.

Although Brian always wore civilian clothes when they went out, he still had to be careful where they went. Some areas were off limits, and he wasn't supposed to be out on his own at anytime, so he wore a wool cap like all the Belfast boys wore, pulled down.

One night after he had taken her to the movies, they stood cuddling and kissing as they had done before when along came two big men.

"Oh, my God, it's me brothers!" she cried, and away she ran for home. They came up to Brian when they saw her run to the house.

When they saw her turn in the gate, they stopped right in front of him.

"So, who have we here? Who is seeing our girl?" said one of

them in a genial tone of voice.

Brian answered, "I'm Brian Tilson."

No sooner were the words out of his mouth than the bigger man grabbed him by the lapels of his coat. "By Jasus," he said in a complete change of voice. "Are you one of the English, one of the soldier boys, you brazen bastard, with our Maureen?" He struck Brian directly in the face as hard as he could, then followed it up with another blow to the head. Brian was convinced that his last moment had come as the big Irishman pounded him. After he knocked Brian down twice and dragged him to his feet, he propped him against the wall. Brian had not struck one blow. He was simply overpowered by the suddenness of the ferocious attack. He couldn't have done a thing anyway. The man was head and shoulders above him. The other brother, just stood by watching and never said a word until now.

His voice was so low that Brian hardly heard him. "Now, me little soldier boy, move yourself out of here, and, if you value your skin, you will not come back. Your kind are not wanted here now or any other time. Mark my words! And keep your mouth shut as to what happened here tonight, or the next time it will be worse. Now away with you and count yourself lucky you got away so lightly."

Brian could hardly see where he was going; he had been beaten very badly about the face and head. He was already swelling up. Walking as best he could, he made his way to the main street and was picked up by a passing police patrol car which took him to his barracks.

After three days in sick bay, he was allowed to rejoin his squad. Being short-handed, they had him back on duty way before his time. (At least that was the story, "short handed.") He was stiff and sore in both mind and body. All his buddies wanted to go and find the men responsible to even things up, but Brian would have none of it. He did his suffering alone.

He had stitches in his head and three teeth were loose. He drew jankers (KP) for a week, then lost two weeks pay for disobeying orders not to go out alone.

The biggest hurt was the knowledge that he had lost Maureen. He took it very hard. Being a sensitive young man, he though his heart was broken. He was learning bitter lessons the hard way, and the bad beating rankled when he had done nothing to deserve it. The hardening process continued. Now he swore an oath: "When I tangle with these Irish bastards again the odds are going to be in my favour, and I will be the one to do the bashings!"

It was only a couple of days after that, that a group of boys stoned them while they were out on patrol. One kid skipped some flat pieces of slate at the soldiers. This kid spun a piece in Brian's direction, and, glancing off a windowsill, it struck his shoulder, skipped off his coat collar, then right into his neck just below his chin. The pain was intense, the blood flowed and Brian could not see because of the tears that came to his eyes. He was rushed to the hospital, where twenty stitches were taken to close the very deep and dangerous wound.

After another five days in the hospital, Brian's attitude began to really harden. He had seen some of the things that could and did happen almost every day, and some of the things had happened to him. He was granted a leave, and with Bob had a few days at the seaside, but was too hurt and upset to enjoy them.

Chapter 6

When Brian returned to duty, he was a different man. Every day they went out on patrol, and most days they had trouble. One day they had more trouble than usual. There was a funeral in the Catholic section and, when the Land Rover approached, the crowd became very hostile and started throwing stones.

Now Brian began to look for trouble. He was drinking heavily and getting into fights with the other men all the time. Bob Day was just as bad and both became known as trouble makers. Brian was promoted to Lance Corporal and just as quickly, busted back to private again and again. Out on patrol, he severely beat a young man. Nothing came of it and, as Bob said, "He was only another Catholic bastard and we have too many of them already."

Early one Saturday morning on what promised to be a beautiful spring day—the sun was shining brightly and the air smelled fresh as it can only in Ireland—the squad was getting ready for it's usual duties on road block and search as they did every Saturday. This was the day when people came into town to do their weekly shopping. This duty was a lot easier than patrolling and getting stoned—which was getting to be a regular occurrence—too regular for comfort.

Bob Dewhirst was showing a big bruise on his left leg to Harry Gibson, who in turn was complaining about a sore elbow he had gotten the day before when he'd been struck. His whole arm was sore.

"T'worst part about it," Harry said, "is that you go into t'Catholic section and they curse and scream at you, and throw everything they can lay their 'ands on at you. Then the next day you go over to t'Proddys and they do 'same. Ah don't know who are t'worst, t'Irish or t'Scottish bastards." He shook his head. "What the bloody 'ell are we doing 'ere anyway? Why don't they leave 'em to fight it out amongst their bloody selves. They're bound to kill each other anyway, so let 'em get on wi' it, We are right in t' middle. For what?"

The men got in the Land Rover and set out for North Street and Royal Avenue to set up barriers. About an hour later, with nothing unusual going on, a message came over the radio to pack up and move as quickly as possible to Donegal Square. A bomb had exploded in Dempsey's Department Store. They were needed to render what assistance they could. They loaded up and took off fast.

It was an awful scene that they came to. The front windows of the store were shattered and shards of glass lay everywhere. There seemed to be blood on everything and the ambulance men were working as fast as possible. Sergeant Polis ordered them to help wherever they could. The place was swarming with police and armed UVC (Ulster Volunteer Constabulary) troops looking for someone to shoot. Tempers were very short. Harsh words were heard on all sides and it wouldn't have taken too much to start a riot. No one had as yet accepted the blame or responsibility. Everyone was blaming everyone else. This wasn't the first time Brian had been in a situation like this. He just got on with the job of cordoning off the district. He knew full well there could be a number of causes to blame so he kept his mouth shut. That was the best way in an explosive situation such as this. They were attempting to calm things down and make the area as safe as possible. As always, there wasn't an officer in sight. The sergeant took full responsibility. At last, a police inspector (when he deemed it safe) arrived to assume command.

It took a lot more work before the area was declared safe and the bomb disposal squad packed up and left. Polis's squad was ready to leave; they'd been relieved. Brian hadn't realized how late it was. They'd been hard at it all day and were tired out.

These outrages took a lot out of the men, and the fear of further explosions, going into operations like this, was always there. Everybody expected to draw the army into doing everything, but there was never a word of thanks from anyone. Just the constant harassment and abuse.

The following Saturday, the weather was blowing at gale force and the officer of the day declared a day of rest and recreation. By the end of the day, Jim Hurst and Bob Dewhirst decided to visit the Liverpool City bar near Donegal Quay, a safe bar in a safe sector.

"Why not come along wi' us?" Dewhirst asked Brian and Bob. Brian needed some cheering up. Maybe this was the thing to do. They all headed for the bar.

It was crowded when they got there. The dance floor was full of young girls, and everyone seemed to be having a good time. The boys managed to find a table after awhile. Jim Hurst, who fancied himself a good dancer, persuaded Brian to go with him onto the floor and separate two girls who were dancing together.

An oldish man was doing a good job on the piano and a tall, weedy young man was playing an accordion; they were playing fast and furious.

Two slender, well-dressed men came through the front door and made their way over to the bar. They looked carefully around the smoky room and then shouldered in beside a scrawny, long-necked character hunched over his drink. "Hi, bartender, two halfs," one said. At the sound of the voice, the character jerked up his head with a stricken expression on his face.

One of the men, an intense-looking man with steel glasses and wavy hair, smiled at the man beside him. "Well, hello, Carey, how are you? It's been a long time since we saw you last. We've been looking for you. You knew we would eventually find you, eh?"

The scrawny one gaped, his Adam's apple bobbed up and down and his eyes looked like a trapped rabbit's; he tried to speak, but the words stuck in his throat—he couldn't get them past his parched lips.

The man with the glasses opened his coat to reveal a big, long-barreled revolver in a holster under his armpit. He drew the gun and balanced it in his hands. "You remember our John? I bring this in remembrance of him. May he rest in peace." He aimed the gun at the man's left knee and pulled the trigger. The bullet knocked the man off his feet. Instantly the crowd scattered from the bar as the man on the floor screamed and writhed in agony. The man with the gun calmly aimed at the other knee, fired and blew it apart. This was the IRA's traditional way to answer a snitch or traitor.

The other man hadn't been idle. He had also drawn a gun and was waving it around from side to side. The music stopped, and except for the anguished cries from the man on the floor, a hush had settled over the room.

"Don't anyone interfere with what doesn't concern them," the man said. "Just go on with what you are doing." The two men turned back to the bar. Without hurrying, they calmly finished their drinks, adjusted their coats and backed warily to the door. They walked out to a car which was ready to draw away.

Brian and the boys were dumbfounded. This was the first time they had seen anything like this happen, even though they were aware that this type of thing went on. They'd heard lots of stories, but now were seeing it with their own eyes, first hand, in what was supposed to be a safe bar.

This happening made a big impression on Brian. The utter fearlessness of the two men; the power that the gun gave them; they way they subdued a big roomful of men (some of whom he knew certainly had to be armed). All done so easily. The impact was not lost at all. In the weeks to come, he gave it a lot of thought.

The patrols ground on endlessly, day after day, accomplishing nothing but stirring up the local people and emphasizing the old cliché: Might is right. This was brought home daily to the locals. They had no rights, no say in the way that things were going to be done. The gun was supreme whether in the hands of the so-called law-abiding forces or the rebels. Kicks and blows were the order of the day. Women and girls were used by both sides to gain their own ends, and nothing was sacred! Yet, the Holy Church was called on constantly by all and sundry. And the carnage continued.

Brian's patrol had had a rough evening. It was now almost eleven, and they were hoping things would quiet down as they gathered in the Land Rover for a breather. They'd been on the go constantly. Bill Costello had a bruise over his left eye that he received from a direct hit on the left side of his face, but he was laughing about it. He tenderly felt his bruised face.

"Only yesterday ah was talking to two of them kids and they were as nice as ninepence. Today those same buggers are using me for bloody target practice, but as long as they only throw stones..." He paused and gave a heart-felt sigh, then looked at Brian, who today was acting sergeant (unpaid). "What you think, can we get some kip? Ah'm about done, Ah'm needing new golfing shoes. These are as done as me, and ah'v got a nail up in the 'eel too. Ah'm in a bad way, so don't anyone ask me to sing tonight." Just then, a big stone landed on top of his helmet and it rung like a bell. Quick as a wink, he said, "There ya are, Sarge, there's the final bell. Ah can still 'ear it ringing."

Glancing at the others, Bill, a mouthy fellow, added in a pleading tone of voice, "Come on Sarge, let's get the 'ell out of 'ere, let's have a vote on it. All in favor of going 'ome raise their bleeding 'ands."

But Brian was aware that he had a chance again of promotion and he needed the extra money. He didn't care about keeping the guys out as long as the word got back upstairs and he got his stripes.

Another hour went by and finally he decided to call it enough. As they approached the barracks a tire blew out sounding just like a rifle shot. Everybody flinched until they realized what it was. Nerves were in a bad way. The night had not been too bad—no guns—that was something to be thankful for.

Tuesday morning found the rain coming down in sheets and it looked like it would never stop. Sergeant Polis, who was bucking hard for sergeant major (everybody was bucking for something), figured that on a day like this everybody would stick close to their warrens. At least he hoped so. He reported to the boys that for today the orders from on high were to stand by. Be alert and ready to move if called.

Paddy May, a nineteen-year-old skinny kid with big ears and a puckish face that only a mother could love, was a recent replacement from Warrington in Lancashire. He had promoted himself to entertainment chairman. His ambition when this was all over was to take such a job at this local men's club. As Pat Phillips said, "The las' time we had a day off, Paddy came up with the idea of a race for lice (which were just too plentiful)."

He'd heated a metal plate over a candle, dropping the lice into the center of the plate. The first one to the edge was the winner. Everybody had their five-penny bets laid. Unfortunately, Paddy had got the plate too hot. And he had fried lice. The result, a free-for-all with everyone in the barracks.

Chapter 7

Saturday night was the one night the boys looked forward to.

They had had a hard day, as usual, on patrol, putting up with the barbed remarks and unpleasant duties. Now they were ready for a little let down of the tension. Private Brian Tilson was ready too. He had again been busted for drunkenness and was feeling the money pinch. Otherwise, he wasn't too bothered about losing his stripes. He knew he would be getting them back. It wouldn't be long, as the men knew he was a good non-com, and he was a good, fast learner. He watched and took the job seriously, as he did in everything he undertook. He was very young, but looked out for the men under him and they appreciated it. They liked the way he looked over a situation before he committed himself instead of barging in as others had been known to do. He had saved men more than once. But some of the guys didn't care for him. They figured lately he always looked out for himself first. He had been known to neglect to cover the backs of the officers in a couple of the rare actions that officers had taken part in. He was not a favourite of theirs.

Later when he made sergeant, he was known to have sold boots, food and gear from the stores. Most of the guys did just that, sold anything they could get their hands on. Still, he never sold guns or ammunition as so many of the other sergeants did.

He was not satisfied with his money making activities and was always looking to make a penny if he could. He had, like all the boys, signed over half his pay to be given to his folks when he first joined up. So he was always broke, but he never begrudged his folks their share.

As lighthearted as young men can be under tough circumstances, they set out for a safe pub and all evening enjoyed themselves, joining in the fun of dancing with the local girls and singing their favourite songs. The beer tasted good. After closing time, it was agreed that they would go around to Bill Houston's house.

Three months before, Bill had managed to bring his wife and two children out to a small house in Springfarm Estates, a housing project maintained for British soldiers and their families.

The boys each brought a couple of bottles of beer with them as was usual. A few girls came along, so it was a nice company and all settled down to have a good time. There were not enough chairs so some had to sit on the floor. Nobody was drunk and everyone was talking and laughing and taking turns singing and kidding each other about anything at all. There was quite a cross section of religions in the room and the argument became heated as more and more people became involved. There was bitterness, but nobody got too upset. These men were on the receiving end of the struggle and they understood the bitter frustrations of everyday living under the awful conditions.

Harry Gibson put it in proper perspective when he said, "If only t'big shots could lissen to a recording of this discussion of ordinary men and women who 'ave no ax to grind and take notice of what is being said, 'ow it is being said, and why it's being said, maybe summat could be done!"

Chapter 8

After patrol one evening, Brian was lying on his bunk reading some old letters. He felt low and homesick. As he talked it over with Bob, they found they both had the same feeling. So being really cheesed off, they decided to go out and find a safe pub. There they began to drown their sorrows. Two young attractive girls were sitting at the next table and the boys decided to try their luck. "Would ya like t'dance?" they asked them. After the dance, they asked, "If ya would like to sit wi' us, we could talk an 'ave a drink an 'ave some fun." Everything was going along real good, and the boys thought their luck had changed for the better when two big men came through the door and marched straight to their table.

"What the hell do you think you are doing?" yelled the first guy at the pretty blonde, "Who did you leave the kids with?" He grabbed her by the arm and lifted her to her feet.

The other guy was big too and he glared at Brian and said, "Beat it, boy, or I'll knock your bloody head off."

Brian had just enough beer to make him belligerent and didn't like being talked to that way. So he came up swinging. The battle raged for about ten minutes, and the two boys really got roughed up. The manager called the police, who in turn called the military police. The two that came were no strangers to Bob and Brian.

"Oh, it's our two world beaters again," said the older M.P. "It looks like you didn't do too good this time, and the manager is going to lay a complaint on ya both, somebody will 'ave to pay for this damage." The two girls and the men vanished and no mention was made of them.

They appeared before Major Welker the next day, and he

had no compassion for them at all. He would listen to no excuses and sentenced each of them to fourteen days in the guardhouse, also the damages from the bar when the bill came in.

Sitting in his cell on the third day of his imprisonment, Brian asked to speak to the guard sergeant. "This 'ere plate that ah am eating off is crummy and rusty," he said to him pointing to the plate. Within an hour he was marched to the dump at the rear of the stockade and told to take his pick of the rusty plates which had been thrown away. One was picked for him when he refused. He was ordered to clean it with only rags and a pumice stone. It took him two days of hard rubbing before he had it done, and his knuckles were sore. The sergeant came to inspect it and would not pass it until it was polished shiny clean. It would be another couple hours of work, the sergeant assured him. "Till ah'm satisfied, boy, you will stay 'ere and finish the job given. 'Y 'ear?" he barked.

The plate finally passed inspection and was taken away. Brian was marched back to the dump again to pick out another one, even more rusty if possible. He had to start in cleaning and polishing anew on that one. He was learning how hard and unfair life can be and also how to keep his mouth shut. But as usual, the squad was short of men and they got out after seven days. Deep, deep bitterness was building at the unfairness of it all.

Some Carey (informer) passed the information that a wanted IRA man had moved back into a safe house and had been seen. This was the usual procedure: without even checking the source, the officers would turn everyone out. Rain or shine, it didn't matter. Nine times out of ten it would be false information. Of course, it was a good exercise for the men. The officers didn't turn out. The locals loved this and would call in false leads, especially on a rainy night.

This night, the full squad turned out; four Land Rovers with six men each. One Rover stopped at each end of the designated street and the other two raced to the house that had been spotted. The first six men ran to the door and it took but a few minutes to break it open and run into the house. The idea was to get upstairs and rout out the people and catch the wanted men, taking no heed of the cries of outrage from anyone. As the squad charged up the stairs, the children quickly gathered together there to impede their progress. They were old hands at this manoeuvre. They had gone through it many times before and had been well trained to get in the way of the intruders and enable their menfolk to escape. They could and did react like lightning. In just a few seconds the stairway was blocked very effectively.

But Brian was in the lead tonight, and these days he was not in the mood for allowing this nonsense which let children block their passage. He roughly flung one child of about ten years old to one side in the passage leading to the stairs.

"Out of t'way, ya gits," he shouted. He grabbed the next one in the way and flung him aside also. There was a storm of protest but, he ignored it and kicked aside the next kid. They moved aside then when he yelled and waved his gun in their faces.

When the intruders eventually reached the bedroom, there was no one there except two women lying in the rumpled bed. Looking around, Jim Hurst noticed that the tall dresser was underneath the inspection panel in the ceiling and there was nothing on top of it. It looked like it had been swept clean. He figured that the men made their leave through the hole there into the rafter space.

Although Brian was in the lead, he let Jim Hurst motion to Frank Kelly. "Up there," he said. Kelly climbed onto the dresser and pushed up the panel to get his head and shoulders through the hole. He carried his flashlight in his right hand. As he lifted up his hand with the light in it, there was a "thunk" noise and Frank dropped down limp.

Someone up above had kicked him in the head.

Hurst immediately fired up into the hole and round about it. The sound of shattering slates could be heard above the screaming of the women and children. "Pipe down!" yelled Brian. He moved to one side to let Hurst climb up into the hole, but he, Brian, climbed up very cautiously after being ordered to do so by Sergeant Polis. Shining his strong light right and left, he could see nothing. The chimneys obstructed his vision. He then climbed right up and moved about walking on the rafters, but there was nothing and no one to see.

The builders had saved a pound or two by not putting in any fire walls between the houses. It was possible to move from one end of the street to the other through the inspection panels. The locals were well aware of this and made good use of it, moving around at will.

So it was another wasted evening—nothing accomplished except to upset the army and the civilian population some more.

Chapter 9

One rainy night, after a hard day on patrol, the boys were talking about taking a trip out somewhere. Someone suggested that a trip to Dublin might be a good idea. It would be a chance for a breath of fresh air and a change of scenery. After quite a bit of discussion, Brian, Bob, Jim Hughes and Frank Kelly (a boy from Batley in another squad) agreed that the next time they could arrange a three-day pass together, they would visit the Irish capital and stay a couple nights.

It was three weeks before everything was arranged and they could go. Kelly, whose father and mother were from the south, had some relatives in Ballsbridge, Dublin, who would put them up for a few nights buckshee and so everything was set.

They arrived before lunch time after a very slow, three-hour train ride. The train stopped at every small station to unload all kinds of different things. They were greeted by Kelly's cousins at the station and made very welcome. They couldn't wait to start exploring the city.

The bargains were very good in the open air markets and Jim Hughes bought some very good fur-lined boots for his girl friend in Belfast and even paid extra for zippers. As he said, "Only t'best is good enough for my girl."

Bob bought a couple of scarves and some knitted gloves and Kelly bought a beautiful high-necked knitted sweater to send home to his girl. They had a fine day picking up things for half price. That evening they had a session in the local pub and had a whale of a time, singing along with everyone else in the place. They enjoyed every minute and didn't have a care in the world.

The next morning they were all up early and set off for more adventures. As they were in civilian clothes, nobody paid the slightest attention to them and they acted and were treated as the rest of the tourists (of which there were plenty). After another good day, they again had a few beers at the local pub and again took part in the festivities.

Monday morning, they arrived early at the railroad station and were told that there would be no trains that day; everything had been canceled. The line had been bombed and was closed for repairs. So they made their way to the bus station and got tickets. Kelly borrowed some money from Jim Hughes as he had spent up.

Laughing and giggling they made their way to the rear of the bus. "Stop pushing, ya nut," said Frank to Brian, "We'll get there, don't worry." They all felt in the best of high spirits.

Two nice looking young girls, about eighteen years old, were sitting in the rear seat. The boys immediately started to try to impress them. They made friends right away.

Noticing the parcels, the girls asked what they were and wanted to see what was in them. Out came the various things which were handed round with "oohs" and "ahhs" from the girls. Then Jim asked the girls about customs. "Are they tough? Do they charge much?" he asked. The blonde girl replied, "I'm afraid they do charge quite a lot from servicemen and tourists." Then Jim had a bright idea: "What size boots do ya take? If ya will wear t'boots over t'border for me ah'll be glad to pay ya." But the girl demurred. Only after a long period of persuasion would she agree. Jim borrowed a pound from Brian to pay her to seal the bargain and have her put on the boots.

Now Frank Kelly asked the other girl, "Would ya put on this sweater and carry t'gloves and scarves?" Then he paid her a pound, too, when she agreed. As they approached the customs shed one of the girls said, "It will be better if we move to the front of the bus and wait for you outside the bus when we reach Belfast."

After the customs officers cleared the bus, it was only about an hour and a half before it pulled in to the station in Belfast. The girls waved to the boys as they went down the steps and motioned to the side where they would wait. It was a few moments before the boys made it through the rest of the passengers. There was no sign of either of the girls. They had gone, promptly disappearing.

Had they been had? "I guess," said Hughes ruefully, "ther' still laughing ther' frigging 'eads off."

Chapter 10

It was April again, Brian's second spring in Ireland. It came early. The fresh green grass was everywhere. What trees there were began to turn green also. The days were getting longer and they were more sun-filled.

It seemed that the squad was receiving more daily casualties. They expected some, after all it was almost a war zone. Nerves were rubbed raw. But to have casualties every time they went out was getting on everybody's nerves and there was friction even between the best of friends.

Everyone had a bruise or cut from flying glass or stones. There were fresh bandages or aching bones every day. Sergeant Polis had been in the hospital for the last three days with a broken wrist and other injuries suffered in a brawl in a safe pub.

Brian had been elevated to corporal, and now was the squad's acting sergeant (unpaid). He took it upon himself to go down to the office to see the officer of the day, a Lieutenant Arthur Stacey. The grapevine said he could be talked to.

Brian proceeded to tell him there was a big problem. He asked if it would be possible to pull the squad out to rest for a few days, to take a trip into the countryside before there was a blowup. Stacey knew all about the goings-on. He read the daily reports and spoke to the men on a regular basis. He promised to do his best to see if anything could be done.

Two days afterwards, as Brian came in dirty and tired, he was told to report to the office. Stacey appeared after a minute and motioned Brian into the office. "I have good news for you," he said, "I made request for your squad to go to the border region for a two-week training period. That's the best I could do. You are to pack and be ready to move out at six-hundred hours on the sixth. This is the fourth, so you have about thirty hours. Here are your written orders. I don't want to put it on the board. It may smack of favouritism, old chap, and I must avoid that at all costs."

This was the kind of thing that was done all the time. Men were moved without notice. They kept coming and going— here today, gone tomorrow. Sometimes right out of the country and all too often in a box, so nobody paid too much notice to them. The next morning they started to get their supplies together for a two-week camp.

Six a.m. on the sixth they rolled out of barracks and headed for Tollymore State Park, near the foothills of the Mourne Mountains, about five miles from the small village of Castlewellan in the County Down. It was not too far from the Irish border.

They set their tents up in a rolling, tiny walled meadow, on the most level ground they could find close to a stream. With six men to a tent and a cook tent, it looked like a small town. It was a wonderful change from the dirty, crowded city. The scenery was breath-taking, and they stood in awe as they jumped out of the trucks. "Did ya ever in thee life see anything so beautiful?" said John Senior to Pat Rowen, a brand-new replacement. "It's like summat out of a story book. You can see why these 'ere people believe in fairies."

At the bottom of the field was a small lake, about sixty-yards square, and the boys couldn't wait to dive in. It was nice and warm at the top four feet of water, but the lake was so deep that the boys soon found out it was icy cold further down. But that did not stop any of them from swimming every day, rain or shine. It was the busiest place for miles around. The first two days were spent settling in and getting their bearings. The difference in the men was apparent from the first day. Guns had been put down and the tension was already eased, although guards were still posted. No chances could be taken.

Brian had been made sergeant. He had a corporal and two lance corporals with him. Richardson was one. This was his first assignment in complete charge and he intended to take the full opportunity to make it a success and further himself. He had watched Polis and the other sergeants and was now trying to outdo them, if possible, to get and keep those stripes. He liked the power and, of course, the money. That was really the main thing—he never had enough money. They were good incentives. Without officers around, Brian assumed charge. The men dug their lavatories away from the tents. By the third day, everything was in good shape. Brian called a meeting of the other non-coms. "We don't 'ave to 'ang around too much. This is not a 'oliday, and if we let down too much the men will be dissatisfied. Tomorrow we'll take a twenty mile 'ike, with full pack." He wanted to take full advantage of the good weather. They were keeping in touch with headquarters by radio.

Eric Richardson, the radio man, had been busted up and down in rank more times than Brian, but it didn't bother him the slightest bit. He was a real happy-go-lucky guy, taking each day as it came and never worrying. He had told more officers where to go than any man in the army. And he was always willing to tell them again and to back it up with power. Eric had spirit.

If he had been a big man, he would have been dangerous. At five-foot-six, he wasn't much of a fighter. Although he was always willing to try, his bark was worse than his bite.

He was the most upset when a man was lost, which happened all too frequently.

The following morning, bright and early, they assembled and marched off, leaving two cooks to clean up and prepare the evening meal. The squad of twenty-two men struck off very smartly and began to enjoy the brisk clean air. When they stopped for break at lunch time, they were all feeling the effects of not being out on a march for some time. City duty had softened them. They covered about five miles of pretty rough going. Brian was thinking of cutting it down to about seven altogether by making a swing and short-cutting it back to camp, but they didn't know anything about the district. They had mapped out the route before they started out from the ordnance maps they had, but the maps didn't show much detail and did not show the high rough terrain which faced them. It would be too hard to climb. They were at the far end of the map. When Brian sat down with the other non-coms to recheck the maps, he found his inexperience had caused him to make a hell of a mistake. The maps were almost useless to show him his way back taking a short cut.

As they pondered the best way to resolve their predicament, down the trail came a young girl about twelve years old, with a beautiful angelic expression. She stopped to talk with them. Frank Kelly, who had people in Dublin and who had the gift of the gab, was pushed forward to sweet talk her.

"Would you be knowing of a short way to our camp over by Castlewellan, on the edge of Tollymore State Park, by Martin Gallagher's farm?" he asked in a wheedling tone as he brought out the ordnance map they were using. "We are camped on this road 'ere," he said, as he pointed to a small cart track through the countryside.

She looked at it and in a wonderful, lilting Irish voice she replied, "I have been that way many times. It twists quite a bit, but I can show you if you care. Would you be paying for my trouble, kind sir?" And she looked at him with an impish grin.

Kelly laughed and looked at Brian, who fished into his pants pocket and came out with some pound notes. He pulled off two and gave them to the girl. "My name is Molly Byrnes," she said. "I live beyond the bend in the road up yonder." She pointed to where she came from. "Come on," she said, "we must go back a little ways and then strike out over there," and she pointed off to the low hills.

Going back a couple hundred yards, she came to a beaten and well-traveled path leading almost straight up a small hill. and they all fell in a single file to follow her. After a while, Brian had to ask her to slow down as the men had a hard day before they met up with her. They were finding the going a bit harder than they were used to. With a light laugh she agreed.

They stopped after a while for a much needed rest and, checking their compasses against their ordnance maps, they saw they were making good time. After they started out again, things looked good. Soon Molly called for another halt. "I have to go make a visit behind some rocks," she explained with a smile and away she went. After about twenty minutes, Kelly was elected to go look for her. But there was no sign at all. She was gone without a trace.

Chapter 11

The three NCOs got together and checked the maps again. There was a trail leading to the left, but the compass said they should go right. After debating for awhile, they decided to follow the faint trail to the left, since that was the way the girl had indicated they would be heading. After going about two miles up and down the trail, which twisted all over the place, they came to a little deserted stone cabin and a dead end.

Brian was fit to be tied. "If ah 'ad that little Irish cow 'ere, ah'd strangle the little whore," he muttered. They had to turn around and go back and this time they took the path to the right. After a further two hours of walking, climbing and slithering up and down steep paths, they came out on top of a small hill. Off to the right they could see—in the far distance--the camp. But they were still a long way off. It took another two hours of hard traveling before they got there.

Not being used to that kind of up-and-down walking made their feet hot and blistered, and every bone ached. They all tottered into camp like old men and threw themselves on their cots. Their language was terrible, and Brian got a lot of abuse, which did no good for his already bad temper.

The two cookies didn't make it any better—they had no respect for the poor bedraggled men—as they greeted them by banging on dish pans, something they never would have dared to do if officers had been present.

They all agreed on one thing. "That little girl was truly Irish. She led us all over the place and knew just what she was doing. Then she left us right where she wanted to, and got paid for doing it!"

Brian thought it wise to do nothing the next day but attend

to their blisters and sores. Then the weather started to change, as it does so easily in Ireland. The clouds rolled up and it began to rain. It kept raining for two days, only letting up for brief intervals. Now the men were soaked to the skin, the blankets were wet, and the stream running through the camp, which had been so picturesque, now started to overflow its banks and spread all over the place. The trestle beds that they had brought had kept them off the ground. With the ground getting soft, they began to tip the men out, so most of them elected to pile in and sleep in the trucks—like so many sardines.

The grumbling and arguing started anew. What began as a nice break was now a fiasco and Brian was blamed for everything. He had a hard time maintaining discipline. He was really learning how "good" it was to be in charge.

When they had been there a week, things improved a little. The weather took another turn and was sunny and warm again. It wasn't long before things dried out and peace came back to the camp.

Just as it got light one morning, Brian found he had rolled off the trestle bed during the night and then had rolled out of the edge of the tent up to the guy wires. A sheep was giving his face a good licking. Looking up, he saw that hairy face and got the fright of his life. He jumped up screaming and yelling, "Wha' the 'ell is going on?" The sheep were all over the field. The sentry stood about twenty feet away and had not done a thing to drive the sheep away. He watched it wander over and lick Brian's face. The sentry got a big charge out of it until Brian, in his bare feet and underwear, chased him out of the field.

The lavatories were off to one side in a corner of the field, and the rule was that every time they were used, the user put a shovel of dirt in the hole. When the hole was full, another was dug. A canvas screen was put around the hole and a piece of two-by-four wood was supported by braces above the hole so the user could sit there and be comfortable while he meditated.

Tom Rogers, a big man, over six feet, had a run-in with Bill Costello, who though quite a bit smaller than Rogers, was street-wise and not about to let anyone beat up on him. Costello's run-in with Rogers rankled him so he gave quite a bit of thought to getting even.

The boys were playing cards by lamplight, and Rogers was having a good run and had won a nice sum. He had the money in his pockets and had started out for the loo, when Costello asked his good buddy, Andy Slack, to "talk to Rogers and 'old 'im up for just a couple of minutes until ah come back, will ya?" Slack knew there was something up and was always ready for a joke, so he asked Rogers to change some notes for him. But Rogers wouldn't stop for long. He was in too much of a hurry and charged out of the tent as fast as he could, bound for the loo, with Andy and a couple of others right behind. Andy had tipped them something was brewing. Tom rushed into the closed canvas area, and then there was a roar of "Ahhh!" as the canvas collapsed. In the dim light, Tom Rogers' feet could be seen sticking up in the air.

He was on his back in the hole.

Costello had loosened the supports of the holding bar, and as soon as Rogers put his weight against it, it had given way and dumped him in the hole. He was yelling all kinds of blue profanities.

"Ah swear ah'll kill that bastard Costello as soon as ah get my bloody 'ands on 'im." He knew right away who had done it to him. The money in his pockets had fallen out and was in the hole. Everybody was laughing and screaming and thumping each other with glee at poor Tom's downfall. It was too dark to do anything other than pull him out, and the pithy remarks were not exactly complimentary. First he had to go downstream to clean off, and then come back next morning to recover his money. He spent the next day down stream doing a lot of washing. The boys got a lot of charge out of this bust up, but Rogers was biding his time.

It was evident that the men were feeling better from the tricks that were being played. They were like big kids trying to outdo each other. At eighteen and nineteen years old, which the majority were, it didn't take much to get them going; they were all so very young.

The strains had all gone away, at least for the time being. Costello got out of bed soon after to find his boots half full of mashed leftovers from the previous night's meal, but he didn't find out until he had tried one on. Another time he had his big toe tied to the bed.

Brian got out of bed one morning, pulled on his socks and then fastened up one boot. Then he reached for the other and pushed in his foot and got the most excruciating pain in his toes. He let out such a yell it could be heard five miles away.

"What 'appened, Sarge?" said Costello as he stood there, all so very solicitous. It was obvious he was the one who had packed paper into Brian's boot. They didn't get along at all. All the time Brian was being reminded that Costello had it in for him, and never missed a chance to nail him with something unpleasant.

Everybody got real careful where they were stepping, or turning in but it was all in a good cause, to lighten things up. This was what was needed to ease the pain of everyone's wounds and the loss of good friends. They never knew whose turn would come next. It was good not to have the officers around, too.

Chapter 12

Saturday morning the men decided to have a trip to the village of Castlewellan to get some cigs and chocolates. It was only about three miles down the road, which was no more than a cart track, so into the trucks they climbed and set out, singing and all ready for a good time. They parked the trucks in the village square and walked around.

As Bob and Brian stopped to enter a shop doorway, the door was slammed and locked in their faces. The same thing happened all the way down the street. No one entered a single shop. The people they encountered walking down the street just stared with hostile eyes. It was made very obvious that they were not welcome.

They saw a pub and went inside to get a beer. No one was behind the bar and, although they waited almost ten minutes, no one came to serve them. In the corner were two elderly men drinking their beer. They just looked at Bob and Brian without changing expression or speaking a word.

Brian took a flying kick at a stool, smashing it against the wall. He then swept the bar of a number of glasses and walked out. As Bob came out the door, he kicked the spokes out of the wheel of a bicycle leaning against the wall and picked up the bike and slammed it against the wall.

There was the crash of breaking glass as a shop window shattered in the distance. Brian rounded up the men.

As they walked to their trucks, a priest came running up. "I protest," he said breathlessly, "please do not do damage here in the village. The people here are terrified. You have come here, armed to the teeth, they do not know what to expect. Please, no more!"

Brian was enraged. Fighting to keep his temper, he answered shortly, "Rev, we didn't come 'ere seeking trouble. We just come to buy cigs and chocs, and we're about to leave."

As they drove away, they were showered with stones along the road. It was not a good experience.

Two days later, Brian awoke early and couldn't find his boots. He left them underneath his bed as usual when he turned in. He thought right away someone was having him on and would get a charge out of seeing him search for them.

Like all the men, he had a spare pair. Pulling them out of his kit bag, he put them on, wondering for a moment which would be the best way to handle this. He decided he would say nothing for the time being, just keep his eyes open and see who was the culprit.

As he approached the mess tent, the cook began to bang on one of his pots to awaken the men. They soon begin to mill around, and then the clamour arose. "'Eh, 'ave you got my bloody boots?" he heard a voice say, and another voice, "Come on, cut the shit. Me boots are missing!" It was soon evident that every pair of boots (except the spares in the kit bags) were gone.

Brian called to the sentries, who had not seen or heard a single thing. He quickly organized a count up of all the guns and equipment and then the clothing.

The cooks and two helpers kept their guns in the trucks. These four guns and a good deal of ammunition were missing. It could not be established right away just how much. The two sentries and the cooks were the only ones who had their boots except for the spares. Jackets which had been hung up to dry were gone as were spare socks, underwear and towels.

Everybody's pockets had been picked clean. And when the food stocks were checked, all kinds of shortages were found. Even the spare generator was gone.

Somebody had been very busy. It must have been quite a gang. Nobody had heard or seen a thing. Lance Corporal Thomas said to Brian, "Well, 'ow does it feel to be a private again? It won't take us long to get used to it. We're going to catch 'ell, with a capital H, ah can tell ya!"

Brian now began to organize things. He had his corporal and half a dozen men search the ground around the camp, but they could find almost no trace that anyone had been there. It was a complete, clean job.

They couldn't even find whether the gang had come from

the village or over the hills. The village was the most probably place. When they checked, the trucks they found that the tire valve stems had been cut. All tires were flat. The wires had been removed from the engines and sugar had been poured into the petrol tanks. Altogether a complete job.

Brian was still not satisfied. He had the men out again and pressed them to cover more ground. Andy Slack and John Senior were having a last look around quite aways from the camp, when John noticed in a bunch of brush, a pile of rocks that didn't look like it had been there very long. He pulled away the top layer and there buried underneath the rocks, wrapped in three stolen waterproof jackets was the spare generator. They pulled it out and carried it back to the camp, triumphant. The generator and jackets were the only things ever recovered.

Brian got on the radio and reported to headquarters what happened and asked for tow trucks to come out and pull them back.

Then he decided to go to the village and confront the priest they had seen before to see if he knew anything. He marched his men to the village and drew up in the square. The priest appeared and asked, "What is going on?"

Brian appraised him of the situation and then added, "You can now 'ear my orders. Richardson, take four men out to t'farm on t'left road, search the farm. If you find anything of ours, burn t'barns. Thomas, do t'same on t'right road. Billings, take two men and block off the road at t'end of town. Ah will 'old the square with t'rest of t'men. Now, Rev, if you want to return our stuff we can wait, otherwise we move."

The priest was dumbfounded as everybody moved out.

After four hours everybody returned. Nothing had been found, but Brian was satisfied. He felt he had put the fear of death into the locals and it would be a lesson they would not forget.

The camp was declared over and they returned to Belfast in disgrace. Major Welker was away, and Major Wilson was waiting for the three NCOs, and he raised hell. They all came out privates. An attempt was made to make the men pay for the missing equipment, but it got lost in the shuffle of papers.

Brian was heard to say, "These Irish bastards will pay."

Later, when Major Welker returned, Brian was again sent for—this time he was alone with the major, who asked him for details of the actions. "You did the best you could after the stuff was stolen, and I'm giving you your stripes back with full pay. That action you took, boy, at the village, is just what was called for. I would recommend that you call on this man. I think you and he have something in common. And it will be beneficial for you both." He wrote down the name of a well-known Belfast business man.

Brian lost no time in going to see the man. He found John McAvoy to be a tall, stringy Scotsman with red hair and a squint in his eye. He couldn't tell when McAvoy was looking at him, and it was, to say the least, disconcerting to sit in front of him and talk to him. He was the owner of a car dealership and an undercover RUC officer. He carried an awful lot of weight in Belfast. And he had his fingers in all kinds of businesses, as Brian soon found out, legal and illegal. If money was to be made, McAvoy was right there.

After a long talk, Brian was introduced to some others of the RUC and was invited to some of their meetings. They had many meaningful conversations and from then on worked together on a number of communication projects. At this time, it was stressed that they must help each other to maintain the status quo. Brian could and did let him know when things were happening and he was suitably rewarded.

It was made clear to him that there was plenty of everything to go around and he could get his share. Brian was glad to hear this, and the sooner the better. There were plenty of ways to make an odd pound, and Brian was finding them.

Chapter 13

Just when Brian thought he couldn't take another patrol, another riot, another safe bar that wasn't safe, another stoning or worse, the company was sent to Wiesbaden in Germany. Here the duties were more relaxed, and he began to feel much better.

After settling in, Brian and Bob took a leave and went home. The three-week leave didn't bring too many exciting happenings. He looked up his old cronies, watched some football and met with some pals for a few drinks at the Tommy Wass Pub, one of the places he used to hang out. He ran into Brenda once, and she seemed a different girl. She was quieter and looked much older than he remembered. He just passed the time of day with her. Hard to believe she didn't mean a thing to him now.

Then he had a night out with Terri Rowe, the cause of all his trouble before, and, although she proved as fulfilling as he thought she would, he didn't want to ever see her again. He was past caring too much for any of the Leeds girls.

Back in Germany, the men were trained for Northern Ireland. Brian entered into the training with zest. He felt alive when he was in charge of a situation, and he was placed in charge of a squad working directly under Sergeant Polis.

Polis, under whom Brian had worked in Belfast, noticed the change. Brian was getting hardened. Polis liked that. That's what he was working for; to turn the boys into his own savage image. Looking at Brian reinforced his knowledge that he could do this and he gave Brian a free hand in handling tricky situations, watching and shaping him every chance he got.

Every day was spent inventing new life-threatening situations. That's how they learned that their very lives depended on each man's being able to react appropriately to a given situation. A kung fu course and a karate course were offered and all the men accepted. Brian became quite a kung fu operator—the instructor was very much impressed with his ability to perform intricate disabling and life-threatening manoeuvres.

There was time for fun and recreation. In the little town of Mainz, a short distance from the training camp, they spent their time off drinking beer and having a good time with the local girls.

One early evening, as Brian stood outside the beer hall talking to one of the girls, a blonde, blue-eyed beauty came up and joined the conversation. After awhile, the first girl walked away. The other girl, who introduced herself as Gerta, said quietly, "Mr. Tilson, I have been asked to bring you to meet a good friend. He is sitting in his car in the parking lot. I didn't wish to attract attention. I still don't, so could we just walk over there, please? You have a mutual acquaintance in John McAvoy in Belfast."

They walked to a big Daimler parked on the edge of the lot, and Gerta opened the rear door and motioned Brian inside. There he saw a man with the biggest shoulders he had ever seen. When he shook hands, he thought he had the biggest hands, too. The big man spoke in a pleasant voice with just the faintest trace of a German accent.

"Good evening, Brian. I can call you that. I have heard so much about you that I feel I have known you for a long time. Thank you, Gerta. That will be all." She walked away.

"I have some very interesting business to talk to you about, Brian," said the man," and I think we can do it better if we take a short ride. There will be less chance of interruptions. If you have no objection."

As they drove away, he resumed, "My name is Paul Ante. You were recommended to us by a very good source. I received some good reports about you from various people, mostly from Northern Ireland. I am in need of a good man who can be trained in the art of disposing of undesirables, who can keep his mouth shut and obey orders, however unpleasant or obnoxious. A man who is steady under fire and can think for himself. And one who is looking for the better things in life. Have I got the right man?"

"We are a rather unique organization. We deal in services and I believe the only one of its kind in the world. We correct mistakes in ways that are not always lawful, as you have done things that were not exactly lawful yourself. Right? We attempt to render justice when the proper authorities fail to do so. We feel we must stop this erosion of public trust by disposing of these lawbreakers by any means possible. Need I say more?" He paused again, and Brian nodded. "I can assure you the pay is very good and we take care of our operators. It is a lifetime commitment, and sometimes people get killed who are in no way involved. That is part of the business. Sometimes that can't be helped. Your being a military man familiar with weapons helped us in our decision to approach you." He shrugged his wide shoulders, "So be it."

Brian asked, "Ah reckon there will be no contracts or owt like that? Will there be written orders or signed orders? Will there be regular wages or as t'job is done? If ya can tell ma all about that, ah doan't need to think it over. Ah'm lucking to better mesen an will be glad to be a part of ya'r company."

Mr. Ante clapped him on the shoulder, "I didn't think I had made a mistake when I chose you. Welcome!"

They rode for about another thirty minutes while Mr. Ante filled him in on his duties. Security always came first. Brian would attend a few briefings at different places to get familiar with the workings of the company. A system of communications could be worked out. The man he would take orders from was Mr. Ante, although he would be working alone on most of the projects to which he was assigned.

He was given an emergency phone number where he could discuss any changes, or if needed, call for assistance.

As Brian lay on his bunk that night, he went back over the events of the last few days. He allowed himself to soar. He had no illusions as to what he was about to do, nor with what kind of people he was becoming involved. This could be the beginning of a new life altogether, free from the grinding poverty of his former life. He could get his mam and dad a lot of things and help his sister. He could have the easier life of which he had seen so little: travel, fast cars, easy women, and the wonderful living that only plenty of money can bring. And he was going to go all the way for it.

He had heard it said that you get one chance in life; this could be it. What did he have to lose? This was going to be a new

Brian Tilson, one far removed from the naive young labourer of Mr. Crawford. That boy had ceased to be. In his place was a calculating, grasping young man with a purpose, who was going to look out for Number One.

He had seen that the law looked the other way for people with money and those who grabbed and bluffed. At first he had not been able to believe what he saw, but he had seen so much manipulation and abuse of power that he couldn't help but be impressed. He began to think, "Why shouldn't I get my share?" And now it appeared that the chance had come. It all seemed so easy.

Brian, thus, had no qualms as to what was to become of him. He thought he was prepared to take his chances. From now on, he was going to prepare for when he would finish his army time. He had signed up for three years and had done more than half of that. Before long he would be asked if he was staying. He sure as hell was not, and after the last leave he wasn't going back to Leeds. That dump was definitely out. No, there were much better places to go for Brian Tilson.

The next few days he gave a lot of thought to his buddy, Bob. He looked at him in an abstract way, weighing up whether Bob would fit in to the way of life that he was now aiming for. He came to the conclusion that he would not. Bob was too soft, but he did know another fellow in the squad who would fit in to a degree and who could be used.

Len Roberts was from Castleford. He was a rough, pushy type who had no trouble breaking a man's arm in a mild quarrel. He had done this at home and had enjoyed being in a couple of near riots at football matches. He was a born troublemaker, and although on the small side (he was only five foot nine and weighed about eleven stone, six pounds), he made up for his lack of size with his ferocious bearing and brusque manner of speech. The way he carried himself denoted he was ready to fight the world.

Brian carefully watched Len for awhile and spoke to him about various things. He found him to be totally without scruples. He was always in debt and was an accomplished liar and cheat, just the type of man Brian thought he could use if ever he needed help.

He began to make friends with Len. Bob, who could not see any reason to talk to the man, outside of their army duties, was dismayed.

Chapter 14

The company's orders came through for another tour of duty in Northern Ireland. Brian met with Mr. Ante and was given an address in Belfast where he would receive his mail. He was told to burn each letter after reading it. No correspondence was to be taken out of the house under any circumstances. Mr. Ante made it clear that nothing was to be left to chance. Brian understood the risks involved.

The company had been back in Belfast only three days when big trouble began. On their second patrol of the day their Land Rover had been set on fire by fire bombs. Brian received a small burn on his wrist, which didn't improve his temper. The next night, the squad was patrolling Tate Street, a mean little back street in the Catholic section, when a shot rang out. On full alert, guns were cocked. Brian spotted a man running from a house. He called out, "'Alt!" But the man kept running. Brian calmly shot him. The man fell as though pole-axed. Len ran up and turned him over.

"'E's dead as a doornail," he called out to Brian. "Serve the dumb Catholic bastard right. 'E shouldn't be running abart at neet anyhow."

Brian felt good about his shooting. He was getting very accurate. At this rate he could very well apply to join the rifle team, he thought. He hadn't had much as a target to shoot at either.

After three days, he had a break from duty and time to check with the Davis Street address for his company mail. The letter he was expecting was waiting for him. He opened it and read that in a few days he would have an assignment.

His orders were simply a one-page letter of instruction. A

Mr. Jim McGovern of 15 Thurston Street was acting as a weapons carrier for the Catholics. He should be liquidated within the next three days as a lesson to the rest of them damn Catholics.

It had begun. Brian wanted to show Mr. Ante that he could handle any job that the company gave him. He took up his position near the McGovern house as soon as it got dark. He wanted to spot the man before the hit if possible. After watching the house for an hour, he saw a man come out, drawing on his coat as he walked.

As he came close to him, Brian casually asked, "Mr.McGovern?....Mr. Jim McGovern?"

The man half turned and said, "Yes, I'm Jim McGovern. What do you want?"

Brian grabbed him close. There were people walking by, but Brian jostled him as though they were funning, then he pushed his sharp knife up under the man's ribs into his heart. It was done so quickly, McGovern never made a sound. Brian propped him against a doorway and casually sauntered away. It had been so easy.

When he spoke to Mr. Ante, he was told that he might need assistance on the next assignment because the man in question was a well-known gunman who might have a bodyguard. He was known to be armed. So Brian talked with Len Roberts, who agreed to help.

They almost botched it. They went to a safe pub to a spot their man. He seemed to be alone, bellied up to the bar. He looked to be the worse for drink, so they waited until the barman told him to leave.

As he staggered out, Brian and Len followed. He walked down the street with the boys close behind. He stopped to take a leak in a dark place, and Len moved in and got the surprise of his life. The man turned and grabbed him in the groin. Len let out a fearsome yell of pain as the guy squeezed.

Brian put his gun to the man's head and pulled the trigger, but the gun misfired. The man now aroused, hit Brian full in the face with his fist. Although small and skinny, he had the fear of death on him and was not going to give in easily. But Len would not be denied. He wrestled the man against the wall and grabbed his throat and throttled him to death. They left him among the dark shadows where he would not be found until morning. The two of them slunk away. Brian's face was bruised and Len's groin was sore for days.

When he received two hundred pounds, Brian gave Len ten, and he was delighted. "Ah would 'ave dun it for nowt," he said happily and Brian didn't doubt him. He mailed his mother fifty pounds and told her he had a good win on the horses and now had an inside informant. They could expect more when he had a good run. For the first time in his life he opened a bank account. He was on his way. And he never gave a second thought to his victims.

The note with the money made him feel real good.

Mr. Ante wrote," You are doing a fine job helping to rid the world of these people who are intent on stirring up trouble. The Organization is very pleased with your work. Keep it up."

He missed on only one assignment. The man must have left town as he searched for a full week, but never came across him. The result was the same. And Brian got paid. Mr. Ante wanted him to believe in The Organization; that they would take care of him and pay him for his trouble even if he failed to carry out the assignment.

By now Brian's bank account was looking good and he was sure that no one had any inkling of what he was doing. He was on his best behavior, having cut down on his drinking. He figured he got drunk he might talk too much.

He buttoned his lip when he was with a woman, knowing that this was always a good source of information to the enemy. The IRA was everywhere, and he knew that. Although most of his victims were businessmen, two had been IRA high-ups. He definitely had no use for them and no regrets at putting them away. He looking out increasingly for Number One. Keeping his head on his shoulders was his top priority.

Brian's officers noticed the change in him and put it down to maturity. He was no longer the hell-raiser he'd been before; once more he was promoted to sergeant. He tried to refuse the promotion as he found it restricted his movements and he was making plenty of money without the trouble of stripes. They meant much greater danger.

On the streets he would be in trouble with everyone, as a stripe meant an officer to the locals and so a prime target. The sergeants were top rank out there on the streets. Although the commissioned boys issued the orders, that's as far as it went.

"Do as I say, not as I do," was the order of the day.

The address where Brian picked up his orders changed, but

the arrangements stayed the same. When he got to his new place, as usual, there was his money in crisp new bills. A regular payment schedule had been set, plus bonus payments when a special assignment was completed. Things were going well indeed.

Brian hadn't met anyone else from The Organization (as Mr. Ante called it for want of a better name), except Mr. Ante. The orders were never signed. They simply had the name and address of the intended victim, sometimes with a photo. Although no time limit was set, Brian understood that the assignment was to be carried out as soon as possible.

While the squad was on patrol one afternoon, there was severe action. A gang of men built barricades on the streets and pelted the solders for about twenty minutes before the situation turned really ugly.

A fire bomb hit the Land Rover and set the tires on fire. Bob Day, the driver of the day, was alone in the truck and was ready to move when the engine stalled. Another bomb hit inside. Bob was engulfed in flames. Brian rushed up as quickly as he could, jerked open the driver's door and reached inside for Bob, grabbed his collar and dragged him out, all in one motion. He rolled him on the ground, twisting and turning to try to put out the flames. He tore off his own rain jacket, which had caught fire and threw it on the ground. Then he flung himself on top of Bob to smother the fire. Beating with his hands, in a frenzy of action, he succeeded in putting out the flames.

Bob was badly burned, screaming in pain. "Mother of God, 'elp me, 'elp me! Mother of God, 'ave mercy!" he screamed at the top of his lungs.

Since the Land Rover was out of commission, they radioed for an ambulance. It took a long time to get through. The boys bundled them in for a fast trip to the hospital. Brian's hands were burned, but Bob was in an awful state. He'd lost all of his hair and his eyebrows, and his face, arms and chest were burned severely. He never returned to the squad, but was discharged after a long hospital stay. Brian tried to visit him but was told that he was having mental problems and no visitors were allowed. Brian never saw him again.

Losing Bob was very hard on Brian. For days he was very despondent and inconsolable. Bob was the only man in the squad Brian was close to. Now he was more alone than ever.

In his despondency, Brian had something to console him.

He felt he was getting even with these "Toffs" for the years of hunger and privation as a child. He, Brian Tilson, had the power of life and death over some very rich and powerful people. He was also getting together a good bank balance and he gloated over it. By the time he finished his army stint, he would, at the present rate, have thousands of pounds. He had sense enough not to use only one bank. From the start he drew a complete list of the banks in which he had deposits. He didn't intend for his folks to miss any of his money if anything happened to him. He never missed the chance to add to it. It was becoming an obsession! He was going to be rich, come what may.

Brian had no illusions. He'd made enemies and knew it. He realized that someone could catch him him napping and tried at all times to stay alert. He had seen what could happen in a split second when you let your guard down.

It seemed to him that they were losing more than their share of men from his squad, but Len bore a charmed life. Brian had a dozen scars from burns and wounds. But Len had nothing. With a big impish grin across his face, he told Brian, "Ah can dodge better than thee." Brian kept him supplied with booze and drinking money and made sure he was never short. He never knew when he would need him again.

Brian had a good steady squad. Len would follow orders blindly and was never slack about going into action. Paddy May lost two brothers in a fire and blamed himself. He was rock steady and didn't care what happened from day to day, but he paid attention to safety. Harry Gibson and Bob Dewhurst had joined up together and looked out for each other. Both Geordies, both good men, they stayed to themselves most of the time. Bob was the marksman of the squad who could kill from three hundred yards. Nobody messed with Harry or Bob.

Bill Costello was from the Ardwich section of Manchester, a tough section of a tough city. Bill had boxed against some of the best, as his scar tissue showed. He spoke with a slur but was nobody's fool. He hadn't lost any of his street smarts. In a fist fight—and there were plenty of those—he was tops.

Smoky Gibbs was from Salsford, a suburb of Manchester, and was never without his cigarette. He was educated and often quoted Shakespeare. Smoky's mother was a school teacher with high hopes for him. She tried to guide him, but Smoky was very headstrong. Until he met Brian he didn't believe in obeying orders. Brian soon straightened him out.

Pat Phillips was the son of a sergeant major and wanted in the worst way to emulate his father. He was strictly all army. He was working toward a commission and had been promised one if he could reach a certain point. They all knew it was a waste of time. In the British Army, without the old school tie and higher education in public school, a commission is out of reach for a graduate of grammar school. A and O levels count for nothing.

You had to belong to the elite. But Pat was on his toes and did everything right. As he said, "Ya never know."

Another day, they took off on a stop-and-search mission. The squad set up a check point on Thomas Street in the Catholic section. Smoky was on point and Brian put Len and Bill to search parcels. An informer said that bomb materials would be coming through. The search was to be conducted with extra care.

Brian moved around the Land Rover, keeping everyone in sight. All shapes and sizes came through, and the day dragged on. The men were tired out. As an old lady came to the line, she struggled with Bill when he started to reach into her big carpet bag. She squalled, "Get your hand off my stuff." Immediately a number of young men gathered and started pushing and shoving. Brian saw one young man grab a parcel from the old lady and take off running. He raised the alarm.

"Stop that man," he yelled, pointing at him. "Smoky, grab that bag from the old lady." He wasn't quick enough. Another young fellow had her bag and was high-tailing it down the road. A small white-haired man on the edge of the crowd now fell to the ground. A lady standing near him cried out, "He's having a heart attack!" Instantly some young children started chanting, "Help, help our da is having a heart attack." It all happened so fast and smoothly that it smacked of long practice.

Brian was furious; he had almost had the bag in his hand. He was sure it was bomb material and he had lost it. When he made his report, he was chewed out and threatened with the loss of his stripes again for not shooting the man running away. That the street was crowded didn't matter. He should have shot the man. He was getting awfully sick and tired of these half-assed officers climbing all over him every time anything went wrong.

Now and again the sergeants met to discuss strategy and

of course how they could keep the officers off their backs. At one of these sessions, Brian had a long talk with Polis. Brian just knew that Polis had something going on the side. Could it be the same thing that he was doing?

Polis told Brian that he was not signing on any more. He would be leaving the service soon and wanted Brian to keep in touch with him. He said, "Ah 'ave some connections an we can see abart working summat together in t'security line." Brian had no intentions of working any such thing with Polis, nothing so humdrum. He had made a decision in Germany.

Brian thought that when he got out he would buy into a small business and do some traveling. He had already contacted Mr. Ante about whether The Organization had any plans for him when he was free. Brian liked the way they did business—neat and tidy, no loose ends, and a minimum of fuss. And the money was very good. He hadn't received any complaints about the way he did things. Until now he hadn't needed to ask for help. In a tight corner he used Len, but that was different. He had no idea how big The Organization was. He'd had to take Mr. Ante's word on that. He only knew a couple of members so he had no means of checking on them. He had to take all of them at their word.

With things the way they were in Northern Ireland, a whole lot of grievances were being settled; business partnerships were terminated with one partner found dead; husbands were disappearing, wives too. There were people killed every night. No one was safe. This was anarchy. It was obvious to everyone that killers were busy.

Chapter 15

Brian completed his reports after what had been an unusually quiet day. He was bored and went out looking for some female company. He'd barely spoken to a female for a week. Brian headed to a safe pub run by Tom Brady. Sitting in a corner of the back room, he was joined by Rita Gavan, whom he had met the week before. He was taken by her light chatter, as well as her ample bust. For such a small girl, about five-foot-three, she was big-busted (he guessed about size forty-eight).

Rita enjoyed a good joke and a good time. After a few drinks she quickly got Brian aroused and suggested they go to her place. They sneaked out the back way, strictly against regulations, and headed for Rita's place three streets away. Brian wasn't one to bother about regulations when it suited his purpose. It was only about half a mile to her bedsitter and her sofa bed.

It didn't take long for Brian to get the sofa out and ready. They jumped in right away and soon relieved their pent-up desires. The wheezing and panting subsided, and they lay back exhausted. Rita slid off the bed, opened a drawer and drew out a small package, tore it open and spilled the powder on to the top of the stand. Then, taking a little tube, she inhaled some of the powder. She gave the tube to Brian and said, "Okay, swaddie, draw on that. That will put new life into you."

When he finally awoke the next morning, his head was splitting. He felt like he was dying. He groaned long and very deeply. Rita got out another package, and the pain cleared like magic.

They talked over eggs, bacon, tea and toast. Eventually the talk came around to the army. Rita hadn't been in the district very long and was trying to get information to better her business. She wanted the names of potential customers for both her bedroom business and cocaine. Sergeant Polis's name came up and Rita tried to cover it up, but Brian pounced on it.

He grabbed her by the arm and twisted it when she denied she knew him. Brian thought Polis had beaten him to a new piece in the neighbourhood. That didn't bother him too much; the sergeants made it a policy that any information from new girls was to be shared among them all. Here was one who could be the enemy, and they had heard nothing from Polis.

When Rita finally broke down, she really shook Brian. She told him that Polis was her supplier of cocaine. So that was his game! He would be making ten times what Brian was making. He kept saying over and over, "T'ol bastard, and 'e never let on!" He was mortified, but not for long.

Brian waltzed Rita around the room until she was dizzy. She thought he had gone crazy even though he looked all right. He looked pleased with himself, too. She thought to herself, "How do ya explain men? One minute they love you to death and the next minute they are trying to break your arm. I give up." She said with a sigh, "If ya put ye'r 'ands on me again, ah'll cut ye'r damned 'eart out." She wasn't without fire. On her own since fourteen, now at twenty-two, she wasn't about to be beaten up by a half-assed soldier boy.

Brian did a lot of thinking before he returned to the barracks later that day. He couldn't make up his mind whether to confront Polis and let him know he knew about the cocaine, and demand a share of the business, or keep quiet and take it over after Polis left.

Polis had said he would not be staying much longer and he would surely be looking for someone to take it over from him. Brian wondered if the risks were worth it, to stay right here in the district. Without the confines of the army, Brian thought he would be free to move about in his own business, doing more in his line of work, recruiting his own force, working in or out of The Organization.

Brian's mind leaped as he thought about all the possibilities. With his ins in the RUC, he felt he could soon muscle his way into the local drug scene. He again allowed himself to soar. He was already rich from the money he pulled in from The Organization, but he wanted a lot more. And with the situation in Northern Ireland, it would be a long time before things settled down there. It wouldn't take a lot to get trouble started again. In their conferences, the sergeants often spoke of what caused the conflict. It was the consensus of those present that the businessmen wanted the troubles. They agreed that, irrespective of race or religion, the day THEY decided to call a halt, that would be the last day of causalities. Most of the casualties were inflicted by outsiders intent on settling old scores, business or otherwise.

At the sergeants' next meeting, Brian spoke with Polis and made arrangements to meet at Polis's apartment for a private talk.

Chapter 16

Brian had been impatient for a private meeting with Polis. When he arrived at the apartment, he was ready for the drink that was offered and anxious to bring up the reason for the meeting.

With a few drinks under their belts, Brian broached the subject.

"Well, we know why I'm 'ere?"

"Yes, right, let's get on wi' it," said Polis.

Brian decided to use the direct approach. He wanted to know about Polis's customers and the direct approach would rattle him. It did. Polis was amazed. He had no idea Brian knew of his activities and demanded to know how he got the information, and why he was sticking his nose into his business.

"Now lissen, mite. It's no concern of your'n. 'Ow the 'ell ya got to know dun't matter. Dun't think for a minnit ya can butt in. Ah'm telling right na, keep ya'r nose out of my action. (Polis was London born and bred, but after fifteen years living every day with Yorkshire men, he spoke as much Yorkshire as they did and got it mixed with his London accent.)

Now they faced each other as enemies, and Polis was mad. He knew what Brian was after. He knew Brian was money-hungry and he knew full well that Brian was utterly ruthless. He had been one of the people who made him that way. He knew deep down, tough as he was, here was someone just as tough—someone who would kill for the price of a pint of beer. He shuddered to think what he had created.

But he had no intention of knuckling down to Brian and came back at him again. "Ah won't tell ya again. Ah 'ave some very good connections 'ere, and ah've worked a long time to get em. and ah don't intend to let no 'alf-harsed pillack push me out. Thee or anyone else."

Brian glared back at him. "Ya will be leaving before very long. Ah've no intention of moving in on ya, but there's plenty for everybody. Ya don't frighten me a bit. Listen old cock, I want a share of what's going. Ah can wait til ya'r gone, ah'm in no rush. Either way, it's all the same to me."

Silence. Then Polis said, "Ah 'ave partners. Ah will 'ave to talk to them. Ah'll get back to ya later on."

Brian had to be content with that. He began making plans right away. He decided that he would wait until he knew more about Polis's contacts, then Polis would have to go. Just like that.

Although this was his first personal score to settle, it didn't bother him one bit. All he could see was a bright future for himself. He knew instinctively that Polis was afraid of him and it gave him a feeling of superiority. Now he knew he could move in on Polis anytime he wanted, and he gloated inwardly.

A few days later Polis called him to arrange another meeting—in a hotel. Meantime, Brian went to see McAvoy, who listened to everything Brian had to say.

"These are not our kind of people," said McAvoy. "I will get you a tape. Wear it the next time you meet with them and be careful. We will take care of them."

Brian had the tape in his pocket for the meeting. When he arrived, Polis was there with two men. He recognized Tom Doyle, a local furniture dealer, a small good-looking man with wavy hair. He looked like a choir boy and had a nice quiet voice. The other man was introduced as Moses Sleak, a fat little man with a big beer belly, who was used to being in charge of everything he did. This meeting was no exception.

Moses did the talking and didn't beat about the bush. "I understand you want into the company. I have news for you, boy. Nobody, I mean nobody, comes in without I say, understand?"

Brian looked right back at him. "I was looking to get some action. Like everybody else, I need money."

Sleak spoke through tight lips, "I intend to run my operation in this city as I choose, and we will not take any interference from you. We intend to enlarge our operation and will be looking for some good men. I will contact you if we can use you, but don't think for a minute we need you or anyone else." The look he gave Brian gave him the chills.

Brian turned the tapes over to Mr. McAvoy, and a few days later both Sleak and Doyle were found dead. Mr. McAvoy did not allow competition in Belfast. Reports said that the IRA did the killings.

Chapter 17

In the streets things went from bad to worse. Daily patrols made an effort to keep control and the troops were run ragged. Brian received his mail every three days. He attended to his duties and waited. Thursday night brought a big alert that there was going to be a meeting the following night of some of the big IRA leaders.

The squad leaders were called together in the officers' quarters to plan strategy. It was agreed that four squads would be sufficient. Polis, as senior sergeant, was to take full command and direct the operation.

The company assembled the next evening and loaded into four Land Rovers. The plan was to wait for darkness. Then Brian would take the rear with his squad and wait until Polis assaulted the front of the house. The third and fourth squads would disperse up and down the two nearby streets to be ready to move and block any moving vehicles.

When Brian reached his assigned spot, directly across the street, he saw a fire-gutted house without windows or doors. He called to Len Roberts to follow him inside. He felt that by going up to the second story, they'd have a good vantage point from which to look down into the back garden of the suspect's house. They'd have a good position from which to fire, if needed.

He deployed his own and the number three squad around the end of the street on both sides of the house and then made his way with Len into the house to wait for the appointed time. They were lucky to find they could make their way up the fire-ravaged staircase without too much trouble. They treaded carefully over the gaping holes in the floor. They made their way to the window, through the piles of rubbish, picking up some bits of wood to make their footing more secure. The view from there was good. With the infra-red scopes, they could see everything in the garden.

The curtains on the house were tightly draw. Nothing could be seen or heard from there. Brian took his Armulte off safety and prepared for action. He motioned Len to do the same. Len knelt and rested his automatic rifle on the window sill. They spoke in whispers, but only when necessary. Len checked his watch and raised two fingers, signifying two minutes. Brian hunched his shoulders and grinned. He loved these moments of anticipation. He was completely relaxed and hoped that the lousy Irish would make a break for it. He rubbed his rifle lovingly at the though that he could get at least two of them. He didn't need any more light with his pet infra-reds.

Although it was dark, he could still see. He could make out Smoky Gibbs huddled in a doorway about fifty yards away. Further down was Harry Gibson. He could see fairly well— enough to get off a good shot and to see what he was shooting at. That was all he needed.

Brian waved to Harry and gave him the high sign. There was noise. The curtains moved aside on Number 23, and he saw the back door open. A member of Polis's squad stood in the doorway and then stepped back into the house. Brian and Len could see down and through the door of what appeared to be in the kitchen. Then he saw a man in shirt sleeves struggling with a man in uniform. Suddenly two men burst through the door Brian drew a bead on the first man, aiming for his legs, saying to Len, "First man mine." The procedure called for the senior man to take the first shot. Brian fired off a burst; the man toppled off his feet. Len let loose right behind him and stopped the second man. As he rolled on the path, more men burst from the house. A uniformed figure came under the light in the kitchen. It was Polis. Brian didn't hesitate. He drew a quick bead and got off a single shot that he knew couldn't miss. It didn't.

Brian and Len made their way down to the street. The four squads already had rounded up eight men. The rest escaped into the neighbourhood. When they reached the house, they found Polis dead, two other soldiers wounded, and two men of the house also wounded. It had been a good night for Brian— his problem was solved.

Polis's death brought no inquires; he was listed as killed in action. That was the end of that. Brian was told he was elected to gather Polis's effects together and take them, along with the body and three men from Polis's squad to London for burial. Polis was to receive a hero's funeral. His sister, Gracie, his only next of kin, met him at the station. She was visibly heartbroken.

Grace had never married. With hair dyed pitch black she looked about forty. A lovely figure. She was a gregarious person. She and Brian hit it off right away. She was an astute business woman and began to teach him things about business from the first day she met him. Brian soaked it up like a sponge.

No one who knew them could believe she was Polis's sister. She still missed him; he was her only brother.

In the evening, they went out and met some of her friends, of which she had legions. And they hit every boozer in town and had a glorious time.

Brian had only intended to stay one day, but the entertainment was so good that the next night they hit every pub she missed the night before. He loved it all.

In his sober moments (which were few) he considered moving to this district. He could very easily get used to this free-and-easy mode of living. The booze, sex and singing suited him fine. Through Gracie, he was making a lot of contacts and he filed them away for reference later. He was learning very fast the ways of the world of business, how to use people, and how to take care of those who opposed him. Although young and strong, by the time he headed back to the airport, he felt he could use a rest. (This was sure a fast life.) He'd promised Gracie he would be back. He licked his lips at the prospects ahead.

Chapter 18

It was a big surprise to Brian when he received an order to place Norma Lind on his list. She was living at an address in the Catholic Short Strand area. He had seen Miss Lind a couple of times in the district. She was from New Jersey, in the USA, and was a part-time free-lance reporter working for a number of American newspapers. She was in her early fifties, a nice friendly lady and popular with the newspaper crowd. A Catholic, she had evidently sent in too many articles showing their side of the struggle and was not going to be allowed to get away with it.

He knew the house where she lived, having patrolled by there many times, so he started to make some plans. This was the first time he had a woman on his list. He had a more than sneaking feeling that this in itself was more in the nature of a test to see if he were squeamish. Well, was he?

He gave it a lot of hard thought. Some parts of the operation were going to be better than others, and he may was well face up to it right now and get used to the idea. He shrugged his shoulders. "What's the difference, male or female?"

He could kill Norma Lind or he could say good-bye to the riches and the better life and power he had been promised and was already starting to enjoy.

The last time he saw Miss Lind was in a Catholic pub frequented by the press, so he checked that place the next night, but she wasn't there. Nor was she for three nights afterwards, but on the fourth night there she stood at the bar, talking with a couple of men. She had consumed a few drinks and was arguing rather loudly. He had a drink, then left. He walked down the street away from the door and stood in a doorway to wait for her to pass him on her way home.

After quite a long period, she came out with another lady and they began to walk toward her apartment. Brian followed close behind. The street was not brightly lighted, but he could see her easily enough and hear her arguing with the other girl.

There were a few people walking the street. Brian didn't have any plan of action, preferring to wait to see how things turned out, and if he could get her on her own. As they came to her house, (the door opened right off the sidewalk) the other girl just raised her hand in a kind of salute and said, "Good night, see you tomorrow," and kept going on her way.

Brian quickened his pace and, as Norma groped in her handbag for her key and inserted it in the lock of the door, he stepped up close behind her. He quickly put his left arm around her neck and pulled her tightly to him. As the door swung open, he lifted her into the hallway with his right arm around her waist. She wasn't very big, only about five-two and of slender build—no match for Brian—who now kicked the door shut behind him. Then with a quick upward pull and twist with his left wrist, he crushed her larynx.

There was a small night light burning in the hallway—enough for Brian to see his way to carry her up the carpeted stairway to the second floor, from where he promptly threw her back down. Then he kicked the carpet loose at the top of the landing.

Taking a look around, he placed her handbag near the middle of the stairs. Then he arranged her head so that it twisted against the wall.

He couldn't see anything out of place or anything he missed, so he calmly walked out the door and into the dark night. It was done with a minimum of noise or fuss. No one had been disturbed and not a word had been spoken. All had been done in the space of about three minutes. He felt kind of numb but now was sure he could take care of any assignment.

He also realized that he could not plan an operation completely in advance, but would have to learn to adjust to circumstances, then take advantage of prevailing conditions.

At the inquest, the following week, a verdict of accidental death was returned. It appeared that the lady had fallen because of a loose carpet.

Chapter 19

Keeping dry and out of trouble was the order of the day, but fights broke out constantly among the men.

Sergeant Dawson, who was now the top sergeant, came up with another idea: leave the trucks and do some foot-slogging for a change. Dawson had been getting gripes about the bumping in the trucks—so off they went on foot. Down country lanes they saw big houses and country estates of the gentry, hundreds of acres doing nothing but graze sheep—beautiful farm land. As Jim Hurst, who had done some farming himself, said, "What a wonderful farm this must have been. I can see where the homestead was. I would rebuild t'house right there and a barn there," and his eyes lit up. "Fat chance, all I do is fight to save it for someone else whose grandfather stole it from the real owners."

The third day was rainy and spirits were low. Everyone was tired. As darkness fell, they came to a ruined cottage. They collected wood, made a good fire and, after placing a blanket over the doorway and window, decided a mug of tea was in order. And with sentries set, they felt a little safer.

Their brief meal over, they sat talking in low tones. As usual, Jim Hurst had plenty to say, "I keep asking meself what the 'ell are we doing 'ere. I mean what is the British government doing 'ere?"

Bob Dewhirst, who sat picking his teeth, replied, "Well, the way ah see it, the government, according to the papers, is putting millions of taxpayers' money into Northern Ireland to 'old onto it because the Scottish bastards under that git Ian Paisley doan't want to join up with them there Southern Irish. What ah see is these bloody landed gentry who niver paid a bloody penny for all this, and 'ave never done a bloody thing except collect rents. Their frigging ancestors 'elped bloody Oliver Cromwell slaughter these people. And another thing— when did ta 'ear of a frigging lord's son being killed in action. T'nearest thing was that there Captain Fenmack. They copped 'im, IRA did, at Three Steps Inn, t'body was niver fund, but a bag of rags were tho'to be 'im. For waht?"

Eric, who had just rejoined the unit, pointed to Brian and said, "Now there's a man who wants to be rich. Give 'im all the stripes." They all laughed long and loud—it was a standing joke about Brian. They all knew he was money-hungry and that he kept making and losing his stripes.

But he shook them all up when he glared at his tormentors and almost spit at them. "Ya don't know what the 'ell ya'r talking abart, this bloody land is ahr's, not them bloody Irish. It belongs t'British Empire and we're gonna 'old it, ya mark may words." This was the first time they heard him come straight out and back what the British Government was doing.

The next day was just miserable. It rained from early morning and everybody was fed up. When they got a message to abandon the patrol, everybody cheered. They would be picked up by truck and brought into camp.

As they made their way into camp, they had visions of a hot meal and good shower. But it was not to be. Orders came fast and furious.

"Rush ya'r vehicles over to the pool and change quick. Ya haven't time to do anything but change trucks. Move! Move!" yelled the sergeant. They bundled out of one truck right into another which was fueled up ready to go. They didn't get a chance to catch their breath.

Brian motioned to Pat Phillips to jump into the front with Bob Dewhirst doing the driving. He usually rode in the front, but wanted to stretch his cramped legs in the back. He spoke to Dawson for a couple of minutes for orders.

"Information just came in from a Carey that a big party of IRA men are coming across at Fork Hill, County Armgh. We are going t'intercept 'em," said Dawson. "Ya knows that location so ya can lead 't'way. It's at O'Malley's farm. Don't use lights for t'last mile. Ah might tell ya this is a big un. We even 'ave a lieutenant leading this 'un—when did tha see that before?"

An hour's ride brought them to a rise where they pulled up

for final orders. The lieutenant, who was riding in a rear truck, got out and stood off to one side with Sergeant Dawson, Brian and another sergeant, Sergeant Lewis. From this vantage point, they could see spread out below, O'Malley's farm. It was a big farm with lots of buildings. Tom was a well-known IRA sympathizer. They could see a lot of lights and motion.

The lieutenant, who was pretty green, didn't know what he was doing, so he wisely left everything to the sergeants. Dawson told Brian to take his lead truck down past the farm entrance road so as to block any attempt to flee in that direction.

Dawson and the lieutenant would take the other trucks to the farm, and Lewis should stay put and block the road right there.

With lights out, and as quietly as possible, they moved out. Brian rode in the back, his weapon at the ready; the other two trucks close behind. Descending the small hill, Bob threw the truck out of gear, making it quieter. He intended to let it coast right past the entrance roadway. As he approached the short lane to the farm, a dark figure rose from behind an ornamental bush and made a throwing motion at the truck. There was a roar, a flash, and the truck erupted in flames. The thrown hand grenade had blown up right under the engine, tearing the vehicle apart and setting it on fire. Another came right behind it and hit the second truck, setting that one on fire too.

Brian was blown out the open back door and found himself lying on the ground. He scrambled unsteadily to his feet and through blurred eyes looked around. He stumbled to the truck and grabbed John Burns, (a new man on his second patrol) who was half out of the shattered back door. With a great deal of difficulty, Brian dragged Burns onto the grass verge and returned again to the burning truck to reach in and pull the injured and burning Tom Rogers to safety. Reaching the grass, he dropped unconscious onto Tom.

Chapter 20

Brian regained consciousness on Saturday afternoon, two days after the attack. He found himself looking at a tiled floor. He was strapped tightly into a bed, hanging upside down. He couldn't move a muscle. His body was one aching mass of pain. He felt like he was all torn up, and his mouth was full of broken teeth. "Wha the 'ell 'appened?" He tried to think, but couldn't. A hand came into view and he felt a floating motion as the bed was turned over. He closed his eyes tight as his head swam.

A nice cheerful Yorkshire voice said, "'Ey ould lad, 'as tha decided to coom back. Welcome, ould cock." Brian opened his eyes and looked into the smiling face of a young, white-clad male nurse.

"Ah'm Joe and ah'm gonna give ya an injection so ya can go back to sleep. Don't worry, ah'll take good care of ya."

When Brian came round again, it was dark. But he was in a normal position in the bed. He felt someone tenderly wiping his face with a warm soft cloth; the same blue eyes from a smiling face were looking at him. "Morning, atta bahn ta stay wee us for a while this time." Brian tried to answer, but no words would pass his bruised lips. He turned his head sideways. There in the next bed John Senior sat looking at him, giving him the thumbs-up sign. He turned his head the other way, but the curtains were drawn so he couldn't see who was on the other side.

When Brian woke again, he felt much better. Lying with his eyes closed, he felt someone pulling on his arm. He opened his eyes to see an officer bending over him, his face close to his. "Ah, I see you're awake, my man. I'm Captain Sull..." Brian spit a mouthful of phlegm and blood directly into the captain's open mouth, and the captain vomited all over the bed sheets. The male nurses came running from outside the room. The captain stood back and then left, threatening all kinds of dire happenings for Brian.

Brian asked Joe what happened. When he awoke the first time, he was in a ward with the other man, now he was on his own. "Well ould lad," said Joe, "ya were sounding off abart ya were going to kill every Irish bastard that ya could lay 'ands on, and some things abart RUC, they moved ya real quick into 'ere. Ould lad, all ya'r mates 'ave bin to see ya. Ya'r banna git a medal fo sure, they all say ya'r.

Yer some bloody good man."

Joe fed Brian all liquid food, then changed his dressings. With a great deal of difficulty, Brian asked for details of the action, and Joe tried to fill him in as best he could.

It appeared to have been a well-prepared ambush. This was always a problem since they never knew if they could trust the informers. They had lost three men, Dewhurst, Phillips, and another man in the second truck. Senior had a broken leg and burns. Hurst, Burns and Rogers were badly burned. Although Brian had no broken limbs, they had taken a load of metal out his back and arms, and he was burned too.

Riding as he was, facing the rear, he had taken the force of the explosion in his back, being back to back with Pat Phillips who was killed and had taken much of the force away.

Brian's helmet must have been over the back of his head. It was mashed and this had saved his head. Brian figured he was lucky since he wasn't riding in the front as he usually did. They surmised that his rifle had come in contact with his mouth and smashed his teeth.

Their truck and the one behind them had taken the brunt of the action, and another truck toward the rear had also had some casualties. The lieutenant had already been flown back to England with several burns and wounds. All together, twelve men were injured. Sergeant Dawson was the lucky one; he was the only man to walk away with just burns. Not a single man had been taken at the farm. When the relief squads came in, they found a party taking place with beer and cakes. There were even two priests there and everyone was having a great time. Another set-up!

Joe had some bad tidings for Brian. "Ya 'ave antagonized one of t'most powerful little shits around 'ere," he said. "Ya really put t'cat among t'pigeons when you spit at Captain Sullivan, 'es a big man at Intelligence. 'E wanted to question ya and will be coming back. 'E wanted to transfer ya to section five, with t'burns ya 'ave ya wouldn't last a week dahn there, ah can tell ya. But ar lot will take good care of ya, so don't worry, ould lad." He paused, "Ya's got a lot of stitches and clamps but we'll fix ya up good."

When Captain Sullivan returned later in the afternoon, he didn't get too close to Brian, who just stared at him and through his broken mouth and said, "Listen, ya little puffed-up fairy, ah don't intend to answer even one question. Ah've got news for ya. Tell t'bastards in charge, ah will not put on that frigging uniform again! A've ben shot, burned, stoned and a've ad enough. Ah want to see me commanding officer. Now get away from me."

Three days later, Major Welker paid Brian a visit. By now Brian had been in the operating room three times to have metal removed. He was in terrific pain, and the drugs didn't help much. They took out all his front teeth stumps, too. Brian told Welker he didn't intend to serve any longer and asked about setting the machinery in motion to buy himself out if the army would not discharge him. The major was sympathetic and promised to do what he could. He could see that Brian had been through a terrible experience and had made up his mind that he'd rather finish his time in jail than serve any longer.

The account of the action showed Brian, although injured himself, ran back to the truck twice to rescue his men when he could have run away and saved himself. Several of the men saw it when he did, so it couldn't be hushed up and put to one side by the army as was their usual custom. They didn't want him talking to the newspapers since they couldn't stop or control what he said.

Major Welker had a long conference with his superiors. They reached a compromise. Brian was to sign papers so that he would not disclose any part of the action. In return, he would be given a full medical discharge, straight from the hospital, with full pay and privileges.

The remaining boys came to see him and made a big deal out of what he did when he saved John Burns and Tom Rogers, and they sent him letters of thanks.

Chapter 21

Brian wrote Gracie and told her he was getting his discharge and would be coming back to London to stay. He didn't say anything about being in the hospital, and he didn't tell her too much about his business.

With his strong constitution and the good care he had in the hospital, after six weeks Brian was in decent shape. Major Welker assured him he would be given an honorable discharge within two weeks. His stitches and clamps were removed and the chief surgeon assured him that if he took it easy for awhile, everything should heal well. He had good healing flesh and there were no infections.

Two days later he met with Mr. Ante. He had a long talk, reviewing everything that Brian had done since joining The Organization. Brian told Mr. Ante that he would like to be based in London since he could get to any part of the world quickly and easily from there. "I could use a month to get mesen in shape, then ah'll be available for anything."

Mr. Ante was pleased at Brian's mental and physical condition. He'd expected him to be banged up much worse from the action. He proposed that Brian take a good holiday in Austria and, while there, have the scar surgically removed from his neck. It was disfiguring and could be a positive means of identification if seen.

He also talked to him about elocution lessons as his Yorkshire accent was also a dead giveaway. Brian burst out laughing at the way Mr. Ante presented his case. He couldn't agree with him more. He knew his accent was atrocious.

During this time, when his hands were healing from the severe burns, Brian wore surgical gloves to prevent infection.

This was one habit he kept. It became second nature to wear them night and day. He never did a job without them, and if anyone remarked about them, he said, "I have to protect these burns. I am open to infection." The scars were deep and not pretty.

After a lengthy discussion to iron out the details, Brian left to make arrangements to travel to Austria. He couldn't wait. He liked Germany and Austria, and knew this was the chance of a lifetime.

Brian returned to the hospital in a good frame of mind. He was anxious for his discharge and ready to begin his new life.

Chapter 22

It didn't take Brian long to pack for his trip to Vienna. He was looking forward to it. The plane trip from Heathrow was short and uneventful, and he landed in warm, sunny weather. Gerta and her friend Gretchen were there to meet him with hugs and big kisses. "My, you look very good," said Gerta—he did get on well with the German girls. They enjoyed each other's company a great deal.

But by day they behaved like taskmasters. He was under a deadline to eliminate his Yorkshire accent. Mr. Ante wanted him to go to the United States as soon as possible, but he had to be able to merge better. An accent was a dead giveaway. So he worked hard each day with his tutors, Johnanna and John Botsher. They were retired teachers who traveled extensively. He soon proved that he was a good pupil and could buckle down and do the job when necessary.

It made it easier that the girls were learning English right along with him. Every weekday was a class day. The difference was amazing by the end of the month. He now had almost no accent, but all agreed that it would be better to retain just a little, just enough to make it impossible to be able to guess what part of England he came from. They had softened his delivery a great deal, but of course he would need to guard very carefully against surprises. The girls frequently tried to spring them on him as a test. Brian took the lessons to heart and filed the fine points away for further reference. He had an idea he would need them again.

Some nights, after classes, the girls showed him the beautiful region. As Gerta said, "This is the chance I have been waiting for—to show you some of our beautiful treasures. You must see as much as ever you can. You may never come this way again." They saw great monuments to music teachers and composers—the place was full of museums. They could never get enough of traveling around and showing everything off.

One fine evening, they took him to the Prater Amusement Park to see the great slow-moving wheel. Gerta's apartment was on the Hauptstrasse, and sometimes they went to the Kellergasse, a nearby beer cellar, and ate all kinds of smoked sausages and good cheeses and drank the good beer and schnapps. Mixing with the natives and tourists and having the time of their lives, they had to stay at the Gasthaus some nights. After one extra good night, they stopped at the Sachers, a fine old hotel. It looked so impressive from outside they wanted to see how it appeared inside. That was the night the girls had taken Brian to see "La Traviata" at the Staatsoper.

Strolling down the grandiloquent Ringstrass, Vienna's ceremonial highway, Brian was in a state of ecstasy. He never dreamed he would ever see anything like this. The beer and schnapps were good and life was wonderful. All too soon he had to return to London and prepare for overseas travel. Austria had been a truly rewarding experience. This was the kind of life he was preparing himself for—the kind of life that money could buy.

And he was going, by hook or crook, to get it. A far cry from Leeds.

Chapter 23

Brian sat looking out the front window of Gracie's house. He'd been back in England from Austria for three days and was missing the free and easy banter and living with the girls. He found it a bit rough getting used to London's dirty air after being in both Austria and Ireland. His wounds had not healed well even though the doctors said they would. It was six weeks since he had left the hospital and he still didn't feel good. "Have patience," they told him. He was satisfied, though, with the job the plastic surgeon had done on his neck. He looked again in the mirror—there wasn't a mark to be seen, and it had only been two weeks since that operation.

Brian decided to go for a walk and call Mr. Ante. He needed some action after two weeks of just sitting around. He put on a coat and left the house.

As he walked, he thought about how lucky he was to have a friend like Gracie, but she sure did live a fast life, and the late hours had been getting to him. She had been tickled with his new accent. Luckily, she didn't know about her brother. Brian smiled as he thought how easily Polis had been removed. He had no regrets.

Brian called Mr. Ante and arranged to meet him the following Monday. That made him feel better. Now he decided he would tell Gracie he was getting his own place. One of her boyfriends wasn't too pleased that Brian was staying with her. He could use that as an excuse. He could afford his own place now.

He had a stormy session with Gracie, who didn't want him to leave, but in the end he won and the next day started scouting with real estate agents for a nice second-floor apartment. He soon found what he wanted on Liverpool Road in Islington. The first thing he did was to change the locks—against house rules, but what did he care for house rules!

His next trip was to see about getting new front teeth—his gaps looked awful. He had the dentist make three sets. One was stained and ugly, and the others not identical to each other, so that by simply changing his teeth he would change his appearance.

Three days later there was a letter in his mail drop with a photo of Ahmed Kalisadi. Ahmed was staying with his daughters at an address in Bayswater and would be there for only four days, so it was imperative that Brian move quickly. He was given full license as to how to do the job.

He went immediately to the address, clutching the photo in his pocket, and waited to see if he could get a look at the man and plan his course of action.

After two hours, his patience was rewarded. The man in the picture came out of the building, accompanied by a pretty young girl who Brian presumed was one of Ahmed Kalisadi's daughters. She was hanging on his arm, talking up a storm. They walked to the bus stop with Brian following close behind. Brian watched until he saw them board.

He returned the following day. He'd been busy, having hired an old van and bought workman's overalls. He parked the van down the street from the house and waited. When the man came out, he was with still another young lady with whom he was enjoying a spirited conversation as they walked toward the bus stop.

Brian looked at the lovely young woman and wondered for a moment what kind of heinous crime the father had committed to have someone pay to have him dead. He felt a twinge of regret but shrugged his shoulders. It was no concern of his. He had a job to do and he meant to do it.

Flinging a bag of tools over his shoulder, he followed along behind them with a slouching walk, hitching the bag of tools from one shoulder to the other as though they were heavy. He was wearing glasses and an old cloth cap and his face was dirty. When they got to the queue at the bus stop, he stood behind Ahmed. A few minutes' wait brought the bus and the driver drew in to the curb. Brian had not stopped passing the bag from one shoulder to the other, holding his head down and grumbling in a low angry tone of voice.

As the crowd surged forward toward the bus, which was pulling in, Brian slung the bag of tools into the girl, knocking her off balance onto the sidewalk. Kalisadi half turned to protest as Brian stumbled down, striking him just below his knees. The man waved his arms wildly in an effort to retain his balance, but he fell under the front wheels of the bus before it could come to a standstill.

Pandemonium broke lose. Everybody in the crowd started screaming and yelling. Everybody tugged and pulled to get a better view or to get out of the way—they were all coming or going. Brian found it easy to walk around the front of the bus and back to his van. The tool bag was safely discarded, miles from the scene of the accident.

Chapter 24

Brian's mail came regularly every week, but after three weeks the address was changed to another drop on Euston Road. The drop would be changed as often as necessary.

The first message at the new address told him to call Mr. Ante. When Brian made the call, he was instructed to be at the main entrance of Euston Railway Station, where he would be picked up in a Daimler at one o'clock the next day.

He waited about two minutes on the corner when the Daimler drew up and Mr. Ante motioned him inside. As they drove away, Mr. Ante greeted him warmly and introduced him to the man sitting beside him. "Brian, how are you? I want you to meet Mr. Slovak. He will be working out of our London office when I am not available." Mr. Slovak appeared to be about twenty-five-years-old. His icy blue eyes, hair brushed straight back, and strong German accent made him seem dangerous. He was not tall, about five-foot-seven, and was slim. Brian had seen some of these slim built men in action. He knew from past experience they could be a handful. He wasn't big himself and he knew that size wasn't everything.

Mr. Ante continued, "We are moving into a different sphere of activity, away from war conditions in Northern Ireland and we must adopt different methods. We are extremely pleased with your efforts in carrying out our policies. Up to now, it has been a kind of training process. Now we are going to do bigger things of a like nature.

"I might add that the risks will be greater, but so will the rewards. We will not expect you to work alone. More planning will be needed. So to this end we will be meeting on a more regular basis—that was why I wanted you to meet Mr. Slovak and for you to get to know each other. As you may be working together in the future, it will be well to learn each other's method of operation." Mr. Ante looked at Slovak and added, "Within the next few weeks, we are going to need some passport work done for Brian because I'm expecting a lot of traveling—but all in good time."

Chapter 25

Mr. Ante shuffled some papers and then resumed, "Brian, I will need you to move in with Gilda for about three weeks. She has a large airy apartment and is quite a good cook. I know you will enjoy staying there. She will pick you up tomorrow. Here are all the instructions. Pay your rent and tell your landlady you are going on holiday for a few weeks. I trust that will be all right."

He passed a big envelope as Brian nodded assent.

"You can look over these papers and make arrangements as to where Gilda can pick you up tomorrow," he said. "As things progress, we can go into details if needed."

Brian walked a few blocks and caught a bus to his apartment.

The next day, with only a couple of suitcases, he took a taxi to the airport, where Gilda met him, and they returned to her apartment. It was a beautiful place. It was made clear to him to he could have full use of the facilities—and of Gilda too.

After a well-prepared dinner and drinks, it was early to bed. Business matters were left until the next day. Brian didn't sleep very much. It was his first time in a water bed. He really enjoyed his wakeful moments with Gilda who was very experienced and took delight in sharing with Brian some of the side benefits of the job.

The next day, it was time to get to work. Brian stretched out on the big plush sofa and read his orders. He was to take daily sun baths to build up an authentic-looking tan, and was to sun bleach his hair. If, at the end of three weeks, it wasn't enough, they would resort to bleaches. An authentic-looking tan was essential.

His job would be to impersonate a young Australian coming to England to clear up an inheritance. The cousin of the young man had already met with a lawyer for the preliminary paperwork and in three weeks the other beneficiary was supposed to arrive to terminate the proceedings. Brian's job was not the inheritance.

It was the lawyer handling the case. Throughout the years, he had stolen half the money and knew he couldn't be touched. He had covered himself carefully as he went along. Besides, he was a fine respected gentleman of the old school—very high up in the City of London. By chance, the cousin found the lawyer out. Mr. Ante was approached, and after much discussion, the job was awarded to Brian.

According to Mr. Ante, the top men thought a lot of Brian's work—his quick, efficient, no-nonsense style appealed to them. By the end of the three weeks, Brian had grown a mustache and let his sideburns grow. His hair was bleached out without using chemicals, and he was studying and speaking as much Australian lingo as possible. He planned to say as little as possible anyway. The cousin provided a complete layout of the office of Mr. Arthur Halmshaw (the lawyer). The suite of offices was on Gray's Inn Road in High Holborn, on the eighth floor. Halmshaw's private secretary had her office off his private corridor.

Brian arrived on the appointed day by taxi and used the private entrance along the corridor, avoiding the public suite. He was seen by only the private secretary, Mrs. Pierce. She was an old and trusted servant in her late sixties, who, although she knew more than a lot of the younger, more efficient staff, didn't see or hear as well as she once had. Brian was shown immediately into the inner sanctum.

It was a hot, humid, July day and the windows of most of the offices were open wide to catch any breeze. As Brian walked in, he put out his hand and Mr. Halmshaw shook it. "Ha, Mr. Eaton," Halmshaw said, "It is such a pleasure to finally meet you." He looked at Brian with approval. Brian just smiled. Halmshaw had been expecting a fine, clean-looking boy. He was rather younger looking than he'd thought he would be. To this he gave only a fleeting thought and made a sweeping motion with his hand toward a chair facing his desk.

Looking at this small, white-haired, pleasant-looking man, Brian thought of how he had embezzled all that money, and in so doing, had forfeited all rights to live. He felt good that he was in the position of being able to put a stop to this influential, powerful thief. Instead of taking the seat, he walked into a huge, floor length window, remarking as he looked through the curtains which blocked the view both in and out, "My what a beautiful day. You're so lucky to be able to get such a nice breeze." As Brian hoped, Halmshaw came to join him standing at the big window which was open as wide as it would go. Brian pointed out the window down to the street. He made a remark, and Halmshaw leaned forward to see what he was pointing at. Brian gave him the smallest push—Halmshaw flew into the air with a horrified shriek!

Quickly, Brian walked to the door. He felt the adrenaline flowing. He had done it. He told Mrs. Pierce he had to go to his car to recover some papers he had forgotten and he would be right back. She'd heard nothing. The thick old door had muffled all the sounds of Halmshaw's undignified exit.

An excited crowd gathered on the pavement as Brian came out of the building. It wasn't every day that someone came hurtling down from above. No one paid any attention to the smart looking young man as he made his way to a taxi.

He felt a glow of satisfaction at being a part of an organization which was carrying out such as direct, worthwhile undertaking—freeing the world of these crooked manipulators. He wondered idly how many more operators The Organization employed.

Chapter 26

Late in September, Brian called his mother, who told him, "Your father is doing very poorly. He is losing a lot of time from work, but won't take it easy. Will you come home, son, if only for a short time? He misses you an awful lot." Brian realized he had drifted a long way from home and hadn't been to see them in a long time. He hadn't written much either, so he promised he would come home in another week.

When he got home, he didn't want to flaunt his wealth. Yet, he wanted to show Brenda and Donny Clay that he was better off than any of them. He was torn between his natural caution and his ego. His ego won. He decided to make the trip in his Austin. It wasn't new but was in better condition than a lot of cars its age. With its souped-up engine and new tires, it looked good.

By now, Brian was in good shape. He wasn't bothered too much any more by his burns. They had healed well except for some muscle spasms, which he got too often for comfort. His mother was delighted to see him. Brian was shocked to see how his father had deteriorated in a matter of a few short years. His sister, Annie, had moved to Germany with her husband and children, Alec, and she had had another son, Tim, who was now a year old and whom Brian had never seen. Brian's relationship with his family had been left to slide, but he was pleased to see there were signs that some of his money had been used wisely—new furniture and the house had a coat of new paint. Things did look better.

When Brian went to his old stomping grounds, The Tommy Wass Pub, his old friends greeted him with open arms. They clustered around: "Well, ol kid, 'ow ya' doing? It's good to see ya!" It was good for Brian to see them all, too. They all said how well he looked and that he certainly had come up in the world. He was given all the news—how Ed Lockton (one of his old school mates) had been killed, and Tommy Simms crippled for life, both in Northern Ireland. He felt his old hatred for the Irish flush over him. It had been dormant since he came home and he thought he had out-lived it, but, it was still there. Looking around him, he noticed the threadbare clothing, the general seediness of these people. He felt no kinship with them, as he once had.

When Brian left, the group talked about him with sadness. Each felt a drastic change in him—a lack of feeling. His eyes were now so cold. They could see he had to learn to speak properly but they didn't hold that against him. They didn't resent the expensive clothes—nobody begrudged him his prosperity. Everybody wanted to get on, and he had done it. More power to him. but they didn't think he was one of them anymore. They all agreed the big world out there had changed Brian--and not for the better.

At home, alone, Brian's Mam and Dad talked. They were very much shocked and heartsick that their boy had changed so much. His mother sensed—as only a mother can—that her boy had deep inner troubles—that something was wrong. He exuded a strange feeling. Sure, he had the poise of an older person, but there was something that really frightened her. She was very much afraid for him and didn't know why. Neither did his dad, who felt the same way. After they went to bed, they talked far into the night in hushed tones, finally drifting off to sleep, heartsick and weary. They knew they had lost their boy.

Later, Brian sat down with his dad for a long talk. He tried to get his Dad to allow him to send them more money to help him stay home. As he said, "Dad, I'm making good money and can't spend it all. Let me help, please." It was a lengthy battle, but he finally persuaded his parents to accept a larger sum which he sent every week from then on—increasing it again after a few weeks.

He took his mam out on a buying spree and bought an electric blanket for them. This was a real luxury and they loved it.

Brian returned south, with his mind made up more than ever. He was never coming back here to live. The place and its people were so far behind and slow. He no longer had anything in common with them—or any part of them. It was "good-bye" without any backward looks or regret on his part.

Chapter 27

In their next meeting, Mr. Ante explained to Brian that he would like him to go to Brooklyn, a part of New York City, to take care of a problem.

A Mafia boss had to be "removed" and the New York people didn't want it to look like a local job as they were afraid that there would be more trouble. They wanted an outsider to do their dirty work, and to do it in an unconventional manner. Brian had been picked. As Mr. Ante said, "We want you to start to work overseas and get accustomed to travel. There is going to be plenty for you to do." Brian packed a case and flew out to New York as soon as he could.

He looked forward to this for a long time, but still felt apprehensive. This was his first big step into the world. Still it wasn't long before his confidence began to build. He was just another figure in the crowd, and this is what he aimed to be when on a job.

His passport was made out in the name of "James Gleason." He went to live at a moderately priced hotel in Manhattan for a period to allow his beard to grow. He could not afford to use a false beard or mustache this time.

After a month, he had a neatly trimmed beard and mustache and felt comfortable with them. With his colored lenses and his hair now grown long, his appearance was greatly altered. He had a good long look in the mirror and was satisfied. He decided to carry on with the rest of the job.

He went to President Street in Brooklyn, an Irish-Italian neighbourhood, and rented an apartment. The house was clean, but could have done with a paint job, the furniture was shabby, but the bed was a good one—for which he was thankful. With a good fast-food store on the corner, he didn't have to worry to much about meals, and the tavern on Fifth Avenue had some good spaghetti nights. He dressed in well-worn clothes, nothing fancy, and he fit right in. His information sheet noted that the Mafia men often gathered at a bocce-ball court on Second Street, so he walked over early one evening, just to stand around and watch.

The men were very friendly. He had his left arm in a sling and explained that he had twisted it badly in a fall. He would not be able to use it for quite a long time. The cast was a nuisance, but he was accepted without any trouble. His little bit of Belfast accent helped.

He could not do any bowling, but he could, and did, get into the betting, which was all penny-ante stuff. It was for the fun of it. But he made himself amiable to everyone. One night, after the session had finished, he walked back with a couple of the men and sat down to talk on the stoop of one of the houses. There were already some women and girls sitting there and he was introduced all around. He found himself at the side of a young, attractive girl who said with a smile, "My name is Tessa, what's yours?"

"James Gleason, at your service," he replied.

Tessa couldn't stop talking. Later he asked her for a date and she agreed to go out the next night. It all fit into his plans.

On the following Tuesday night, he heard one of the men call an older, gray-haired man, "Sal." He had not seen this man there before, but the way the men deferred to him, caused him to take another long look. The pictures he had seen of his quarry had not been very clear and would have fit a number of men right there in the gathering. He was looking for Sal Pacanti. The men treated this man with respect and with deference. He had to make sure before he made his move.

Sal would never have stood out. He was just another Italian in the crowd, and to Brian, another check in the bank. Then Brian noticed, right next to Sal, like a shadow, a skinny little sharp-eyed individual, obviously a bodyguard. The other guys didn't mess with him, didn't even speak to him. He looked evil. When Brian heard him address Sal as "Mr. Pacanti," he now knew his man.

Most of the men were middle-aged or older and the bowling was very good. They had played bocce together for years—too many to remember. Most of them were just labouring men. You could tell by their manner. Here and there would be a son who had made it big—all duded up fancy—the signs of good living and money were all about them. These were the hoodlums, the killers and strong-arm men.

When he saw the flinty eyes of some of these young men, he wondered if he had bitten off more than he could chew, and asked himself, "Just what the hell am I doing here? Is it worth it?"

But the adrenaline really started to flow when he remembered what Mr. Ante said when he first told him about the job. "This is top priority. *When*, not *if* you complete this hit, you could be on the way to becoming our main remover. No one outside The Organization will know what you have done. We keep our affairs secret. The top money and jobs could be yours hereafter. There will be bonuses."

Brian knew he was better at his job than any of these men. That would be proved soon. Sal played on Tuesdays and Thursdays and enjoyed himself when he played. The bantering went on all the time. "Come on Ricco, you can do better than that. Your old mother could do better and she is ninety." And so it went.

Brian had taken Tessa out a number of times when she asked him. "Will you go with me to a wedding which is coming up next Saturday. Sal's niece is getting married and he is giving her away. If you agree, I will accept the invitation." Brian replied, "I have no fancy duds. Where can I borrow some clothes?" She replied with a smile, "You will see worse clothes than yours. There are sure to be some weird outfits. This is a nice wedding, but you will be okay. Don't worry. Be yourself, that's all."

The night of the wedding arrived. Brian was smoking the longest cigarette he could find. He really hated to smoke but he was thinking of using a dart tube, which was no bigger than a cigarette. He hoped in the half light no one would be able to tell the difference until too late.

During his last trip to Germany, Brian was supplied with these dart tubes, each one containing a dart smeared with a powerful and quick acting poison. A person whose skin was punctured by one of the darts would be dead in less than a minute. The man who sold him the idea explained that the poison acted directly upon the heart in much the same way as the toxin of the dreaded sea wasp in Australia.

To launch the dart, Brian had only to unscrew a cap with a knurled edge, easy to locate by feel. Then, putting this threaded end of the tube in his mouth, he could extend a telescoping section of the tube . This would automatically knock off a protective cap and lengthen the tube to some eight inches, making it a very accurate blowgun. If the target were close enough, Brian wouldn't have to worry about the extension, but would need to slip off the unthreaded cap at the muzzle end.

A gun was out of the question. These people were trigger happy, and watching for a gun. They lived by it and could think of nothing else. He discarded the idea of a noose. He would never get near enough to use one.

Since he had bought, (as he thought of it), "The Tube," he practiced long and hard with it and was reasonably sure he could carry it off. He tried it with and without the extension. In his top pocket, in full view, Brian had a used pack of cigarettes. In the closed pack, along with some cigarettes were two dart containers. Everyone was searched as they entered the building and all weapons were taken away. He almost had a fit when the body search started, but pulled out and lit a cigarette as they searched him, keeping the pack in his hand. Nobody challenged him as they patted him down very thoroughly. They would have discovered darts in his socks but missed them in his cigarette pack.

There were more than three hundred people at the wedding and the reception afterwards. On one side sat the bride's people and on the other, the groom's, as was the custom. Brian sat with Tessa on the bride's side. She was off dancing as soon as the meal was cleared away. Brian, with the cast on his arm, was unable to go out on the floor.

That day he had taken all his belongings and put them in his suitcase which he deposited in a public locker at the bus station. He did not intend to go back to the apartment again. As the evening wore on, the drinks really began to flow and everyone was having a great time. Brian sat and talked with people, awaiting his chance. Tessa danced all the time.

Watching Sal dispassionately, he saw the little guard was, as usual, keeping as close to Sal as he could, always alert. This was not going to be easy. But he had surprise on his side and could pick and choose his own place to strike.

About two-thirty in the morning, some of the older people

started to leave, and it wasn't long before he noticed Sal and his man, with their overcoats over their arms (although it was a warm night), getting ready to leave. Was this going to be another missed opportunity?

Leaving by the front door, Brian stood just outside on the sidewalk. It had rained very lightly and the sidewalk was slick.

Looking around, Brian sized everything up. This looked like the best chance he was likely to get. The crowd was milling about—most of them the worse for drink—shouting to each other, waving their arms and hugging and calling back and forth. Everyone was in the best of spirits and nobody expected death to strike. It was a perfect setup. He wasn't about to waste it.

At the curb was a big limousine, obviously Sal's. Brian stood there among the crowd and lit up a long cigarette. As he saw Sal come out the door, he switched the cigarette for the dart tube which he had already prepared and had concealed in his arm sling.

Sal was speaking to different people as he walked, turning his head right and left. As he reached the pavement edge, his back was toward Brian. There was a lady between them. He was less than four feet from his car and Brian. Brian gave a quick glance and saw the guard was not paying any attention to him, so he gave one strong puff, and the dart struck home in Sal's neck. He stood a second, then pitched down.

Everyone scrambled to help him to his feet, figuring he had stumbled and slipped on the wet sidewalk. It was quite some time before they realized he was dead. Nobody paid any attention to a young man walking down the block.

Brian caught a cab further down the street and went to the nearest underground station. He took the first train to the bus station, picked up his suitcase, and then took a bus to Manhattan.

Next day, fresh shaven and dressed to kill, he made his plane back to London. He had really enjoyed his first trip to the old U.S. of A. and he was thinking gleefully of that nice big fat check. And that he, Brian Tilson, from the slums of Leeds was powerful enough to rub out a big shot gangster like Sal Pacanti in his own backyard. It gave him a feeling of tremendous power and pleasure to be able to free the world of such a notorious character.

Now he was in the international field.

Chapter 28

Brian had been home two days when he was notified that Mr. Ante wanted a meeting. He was picked up by the Daimler on Charing Cross Road.

Mr. Ante was full of praise for the Brooklyn job. "I received a phone call yesterday and payment for a job well done. You showed good initiative. I knew you could do it—again well done--you will, as I promised, be receiving a good bonus."

Mr. Slovak, who was present, also expressed his admiration for the neatness of Brian's work. "Now you will be taking fewer cases and have more time for planning, and, of course, more money."

Brian traveled to the Continent to take a well-earned rest. Shortly thereafter, a more complicated coding system was introduced, along with a new master card. A stranger would be unable to fathom it. Orders could be left around. It was completely safe. They were sure of themselves, although security never slackened. While on the Continent, he brushed up on his karate.

Early one morning, his mail arrived and he took out his card. Mr. Richard DuBois, a prominent stockbroker in the City of London was his next client. The address was in North Finchley, a London suburb. The following afternoon, Brian hired a van, drove out to look the place over and discovered it to be a beautiful estate.

Nobody paid any attention to a neat, brisk young man in clean overalls and a cloth cap, carrying a clip board. He fit right into the territory. The house was a large, older, three story stone dwelling standing on an acre of extensive gardens. There was a profusion of ornamental trees and bushes and beautiful flowers everywhere. It was obvious that someone did a lot of gardening. DuBois lived there with his wife and son, who also worked in the city. From the information sheet, Brian learned that they employed a full time gardener and a maid, or clean-up woman, three days a week.

He left the van and climbed an embankment at the rear of the house to check the bedrooms. He had been there about an hour when he heard the voice of DuBois raised in anger for about ten minutes. Being only about sixty feet from the house, he could hear and see but couldn't make out the words. He watched through the window as DuBois finally sprang up from his chair, strode across the room and pulled a woman (apparently his wife) up out of her chair. He struck a number of blows across her arms and chest, knocking her to the floor. He stalked out of the room, swaying as he walked, obviously not quite sober.

She scrambled up and then sat crumpled in her chair. Brian could hear her deep sobs for a long time. Eventually she rose to her feet and made her way upstairs. He saw a light go on in a bedroom and surmised they slept in separate rooms.

He felt anger rise in him at the beastliness of DuBois. But then, he remembered what Mr. Ante had impressed on him. "At no time, whatsoever, should you allow your feelings for anyone involved in any of our projects to impair your judgment. There is a definite danger there. You will find it best to follow orders and just do your job."

On the second night, DuBois didn't come home until about nine o'clock. Again, there were loud, abusive words shouted, but this time no violence. It seemed like they fought every night. It was one continuous battle. Later on, he saw another bedroom light go on, and he had an idea now of which one was DuBois'.

The next morning, the weather was beautiful, not a cloud in the sky. When Brian arrived he saw Mrs. DuBois working in the front garden with the gardener. Through open doors, he could see only one car in the garage. He guessed the cleaning lady wasn't going to be in that day. Brian figured he'd have a look around inside while he had the chance.

It wasn't difficult to get into the garden without being seen. He worked his way to the back, entering the unlocked door.

He gave the downstairs a good going-over and saw a little dog asleep in a chair in the living room. It didn't even move.

Then he saw the staircase in the rear, made for it on tiptoe, and headed upstairs to the first bedroom on the right which he surmised belonged to Mr. DuBois.

It was a typical man's room. On the night stand at the side of a king size bed was an alarm clock, two books (one open and face down), a bottle of Magadons—a sleeping pill favoured by physicians.

He checked the date on the bottle and counted the contents. There were ten pills. With a quick bit of figuring, he calculated that DuBois took two a night. He took out two, wrapped them carefully in his handkerchief and checked the windows to make sure Mrs. DuBois was still out there.

Brian quietly made his way back down the stairs so as not to disturb the dog. He left the house the same way he had come in, moving in and out of the trees. No one saw him as he returned to his van parked two streets away.

On the way back to his apartment, he stopped at phone box and called Mr. Ante, requesting a meeting right away.

They lunched together the following day. Brian gave Mr. Ante the Magadon tablets and asked that he find out if strychnine was a quick and powerful enough poison to do the job, and, if so, to get him two pills made of strychnine in the same shape, size and color as Magadon. Mr. Ante told him, "I will find out and call you in three days and give you the news."

Three days later his message confirmed that the parcel would be delivered that day. The supplier assured him that one pill would be fatal. The next morning he returned to his post on the embankment and took up his vigil. He'd wait until he could enter the house again. He squatted down among the bushes in his blue coverall, which resembled the clothes the gasman wore. He had a gasman's credentials in his pocket in case he was stopped.

Three hours passed and he was getting cramped, but the warm weather helped. Finally Mrs. DuBois came out the back door, closed the garden gate and the door of the storage shed and went back inside the house. Brian shifted his position so he could see the front walk. As he did so, he saw her walking down the walk in the direction of the garage with a shopping bag in her hand. The little dog was on a leash, running alongside. Brian heard the car start up and drive away. Now was his chance.

He hurried to the back gate, through it and to the back

door. He quickly inserted a plastic card, opened the door and checked downstairs. Looking through the window, he saw the gardener at work by the gate. He had been there since Brian had come that morning. He made his way upstairs to Mr. DuBois' bedroom.

The bottle of Magadons was still on the night stand. Brian counted four pills in it and a new bottle next to it. He switched one of the tablets he brought for one in the bottle and screwed down the top and looked carefully around. He didn't need to put in more than one as the remaining pills would be checked and he intended to leave no trace. With all in order, he made his way downstairs and out the back door.

When the newspapers reported a big city financier was found dead in mysterious circumstances, he wondered if the wife would be suspected. He hoped not. He felt if ever a man deserved to die, it was DuBois. A man who used his position and power to beat up a defenseless woman deserved all he got.

And then he remembered what Mr. Ante said a long time ago, "Do not waste compassion on these people—men or women. Most of those who we have liquidated were vermin of the worst kind: wife beaters, child molesters, pimps, who live off the earnings of women and children, an Arab who sold children into slavery, others who employ children in their factories at starvation wages and have them working dangerous machinery. When they get injured they throw them out with nothing! Yes, in this day and age! You, yourself disposed of a fine upstanding man who had murdered ten Catholic's, and another who killed a number of Protestants—so don't ever get upset.

"As anyone does, we have made mistakes and taken out the wrong people—but not often."

Then Brian wondered who had hired The Organization. Was the poor down-trodden wife so down-trodden?

Chapter 29

Brian was beginning to feel like quite a seasoned overseas traveler. He enjoyed the change of scenery. Even though he always traveled tourist (as he didn't want to attract attention) it still seemed like luxury to him and he was hoping the next job would be overseas.

He was a little disappointed when he opened his mail. After decoding the letter, he found it was for a client almost on his doorstep.

Edward Garforth was a big shot racketeer and night-club owner. When Brian saw the name, he knew he had a really big one. Mr. Ante had emphasized at the last meeting that Brian was doing the top jobs and making the top money. "Guess they want me to earn my money from now on," he mused.

He drove to a safe phone and called Mr. Ante for a meeting. They had been meeting in the car for security, or for short meetings, sometimes at a safe restaurant. Mr. Slovak, who answered the call, said that Mr. Ante was out of town and that he would was in charge for the time being. He agreed to meet at a private house in Clement Street in Maida Vale, a London suburb.

Brian arrived early, but Mr. Slovak was already there. The young lady who answered the door when Brian rang was introduced by Mr. Slovak as Mary Pearson. She was a recent recruit to The Organization. She had been set up in this house which was to be used as a safe house, a temporary shelter if needed in an emergency.

When Brian was given his information, he was alone with Mr. Slovak. Mr. Slovak told him, "This time, Brian, you may need help. We have an operator there who is one of Mr.

Garforth's personal bodyguards. We want to keep him inside. It would be very easy for him to do the job, but then we would lose our contact with the new man who will come in to replace Garforth. If you need him, he will be there to help." He then showed Brian a picture of Garforth. Standing behind him was a tall, curly-haired Adonis. "That," said Mr. Slovak," is Dominic Carlucci, your help if needed."

Mr. Slovak then left. Brian stayed until the next day to study all the information before destroying it. The time was not wasted. Mary was a charming companion, and they enjoyed each other's company a great deal.

The next day, driving down the A13, Brian made his way to East Ham. Garforth had a big house there surrounded by a high red brick wall. It was on the water with a private dock. A big beautiful yacht was moored there. Quite a place.

Brian wore coveralls and drove his own van. He went into the corner pub for a pint of beer and stood right up to the bar. Everyone was as friendly as they could be in an English pub. Then, to show how friendly they could be, someone stole his beer as soon as he turned his head. He knew the business and didn't say a word but ordered another one right away. "Cor, you can knock it back quick for a young feller," said the burly barkeep with a knowing grin. He never missed a trick. This time Brian kept his hand on his glass.

Next to him stood a watery-eyed little geezer. "Are ye looking for somefink special?" he said.

"Brian looked at him and asked, "What have you got?" The little guy said, "My names Bart and a've gor anyfink, gor any money."

Brian replied with heat, "You've got to be joking. Bring money here? I'm buying, but I want delivery away from this place. Anyway, tonight, Im looking for a good kip. I'm in no hurry but I'm looking for a nice steady connection, know what I mean?"

He asked the barkeep for a bed and slept there that night, leaving his van in the pub parking lot.

The next day, in a steady drizzle, he walked around the district. Opposite Garforth's house was a tall apartment building. He spoke with a young fellow who was standing on the street corner. "Do you know if there are any rooms or apartments for rent in that building?" he asked the kid.

"Y' can buy anyfink ya wants in there," the kid answered.

"Plenty of empty rooms, and don't let the old fart tike ya over. 'E'll charge ya as much as 'e can, so watch aht."

Brian went to the room number that the boy gave him and spoke with the renting agent—a bleary-eyed drunken bandit if he ever saw one. He bargained to get the rent down to double what it was worth. After eyeing him up and down, the old boy said to him, "Ya just come out of stir, ah don't know if ah can trust ya." (A case of the kettle calling the pan black.) Brian had a stubble of beard since he had not shaved for a couple of days. He looked like he wanted to look—someone down and out. But eventually he managed to rent a furnished room on the third floor, right where he wanted it, facing Garforth's house and up above it. He could see right over the high wall and everything that was going on.

He went back the next day to his own apartment and got some clothes, all worn and, of course, his "tools." He didn't know if he would be able to get close enough to use them. He could see this might be a long job, so he got himself entrenched to wait for something to break his way, to show him how to finish the job.

The first morning he was up early. He had hardly slept. The bed was in terrible shape, all lumps, bumps and sagging in the middle. It was the worst bed he had slept in for years, and full of bed bugs, too! He scratched all night. He vowed he would sleep on the floor from then on. At least it was level. He went out to a greasy spoon, had some breakfast, felt a little better and quickly went back to the apartment. He hoped with these conditions he could finish the job quickly and get out.

He brought along a good pair of binoculars and got busy with them. He could see very easily all the activity around the house. Behind it, off to one side, was the beautiful yacht. He spotted Carlucci and, a little later, walking on the dock, Garforth himself. He was elegantly attired in spanking white shorts, yachting shoes and a spiffy shirt. He sprawled under an umbrella for more than an hour, talking and gesticulating with two men. They were about three hundred yards away. With his Armulute, he could have finished off the job right there, but the getaway would have been another thing.

Four days had gone by. The sun, which shone in Brian's window in the afternoon, sank behind Garforth's house. It was just turning to dusk. Brian was thinking of calling it a day and having a break by going out to the movies (he needed a change from his constant watch). He took one last look out the window when the door to his apartment burst open with a crash and in came three big guys led by Dom Carlucci. They had blood in their eyes. Two of them slammed him on the bed, "There, din't ah tell ya," said one big thug. "Ah was right, ah did see the reflection from 'bloody glasses and ya wouldn't listen to ma. Let's tike 'im t'gaffer. 'E will know what t'do with 'im."

They got Brian between them, threw all his stuff into his cheap suitcase and frog-marched him out of the building and across the street to Garforth's house.

Mr. Garforth had left for the day and they began to rough him up to find out what he was up to. They took turns beating him. If they could get the information before Garforth returned, it would be a feather in their caps. Carlucci had already kicked Brian twice in the stomach. Brian, bleeding from his mouth and scalp, was in a bad way. Finally he passed out and they left him for awhile. They took turns guarding him. When it came to Carlucci's turn, Brian came round a bit. Brian waited for awhile and then told him, "Dom, Mr. Slovak sent me."

Dominic look at him, "Don't ya fink ah dun't knaw, ya dum bleeder? Ah've bin waiting a week for ya t'show, and we set ya up good. No one 'ell be the wiser, you dum twat." He burst out laughing.

Chapter 30

Brian couldn't believe his ears. This was the first time since Belfast he had been with anyone else on a job and had been crossed up. And he hadn't missed the "we" so someone else in The Organization wanted him put out. Dom wasn't in on this alone.

The three men now started playing cards in the next room. Brian began working on his bonds. He was in good condition. The beating felt like mostly cuts and bruises, no broken bones as yet anyway. His stomach was sore and aching. There was no doubt he had to get loose.

Then, as he felt the bonds give and his hopes began to rise, one of the guys came in to check him. He didn't do a good job, just pulled the ropes around a bit. When he left, he gave Brian a good belt in the face, making his head ring. "Tha's for even looking at ma cross-eyed, fink," he snarled right in Brian's face. Brian finally got one hand almost loose. Although a bit dizzy, he did feel better.

As they dealt the cards once more, they began to argue. A car was heard in the driveway. Brian heard Carlucci say as he walked out of the room, "It's t'Gov." He returned in about ten minutes and told the other two, "Nick, tike the first four 'ours watching ahr friend and then Sid can tike over. T'Gov will see t'little bleeder firs ting in the morning. Its too late naaa, all right?" And then he added, "Let's get some kip, t'Gov wants to be up early in t'morning." With that he left.

Brian waited. He knew now there was all night to get loose and he had no need to hurry. He didn't want to alert Nick. He knew he would only get one chance and he better make the best of it. He owed those three bastards plenty.

He started to wiggle again and within a short period of time, which felt like hours, he had his hand free. Ah, it felt good! He freed the other hand, but when he bent down to free his feet, he almost fell off the chair. He had a sudden rush of blood to his head. He was so worked up at getting loose he had most forgotten his beating. He sat a moment to recover. There had been no further movement from Nick. He must have dozed off to sleep.

Stealthily, he crossed to the bed. There was no light in the bedroom, but the open door let in lots of light from the other room. Brian reached out for his suitcase and lifted it up on the bed. Working the handle, he removed his darts from the hidden cavity. He had only two, but knew how he could use them best. He had an idea that he was going to test out.

Walking slowly and carefully, he approached the back of the chair on which Nick was sprawled. His dart was at the ready. Nick fast asleep, snoring softly with his mouth wide open. Brian shot the dart into his neck under the chin. Nick never knew what hit him. He flinched slightly and slumped down to the floor. Brian felt for a pulse. There was none, so he reached under Nick's chin and pulled out the tiny dart, very, very carefully and inserted it back in the tube.

He was going to take a big gamble that there was still enough poison on the tip to kill another man. He had to try it.

He made his way down the passage, which was lit by a single small light set up in the wall to the kitchen. Brian had Nick's gun tucked in his waistband, just in case he needed it. He hoped he didn't have to use it. Guns made too much noise and alerted everyone and he didn't know if he was a good enough shot to shoot it out with these guys. He carried his dart in his left hand. After he had a good drink of water at the sink in the kitchen and wiped the blood away from his face, he felt better.

He looked into the first bedroom door he came to. There was Dom on his back, snoring his head off, looking as innocent as a baby, and in the adjoining bed was Sid. He could wait for them. Their turn was coming for sure.

He went further down the passage, opened the second door very quietly and saw the room was empty. He went on to the next one, again turning the knob very gently, without making any noise. He peeped in and saw, with the help of a nightlight on the bedstand, there side by side in a big king-sized bed were

Mr. Ted Garforth and his wife, fast asleep. Brian had his dart ready as he crept to Garforth's side. Very gently, he blew the dart into the exposed neck. Garforth just sighed and was still. Brian retrieved this dart also and put it back in the tube. He handled it carefully after checking Garforth to make sure he was dead.

Retracing his steps to the other bedroom, Brian picked up a gun which was on the nightstand. After checking it to make sure it was loaded, he approached Sid and blew the first dart that he had retrieved into Sid's neck. Sid jerked, half sat up and gurgled, "Ahh..." then fell back and was still. As quickly as he could, Brian turned to Carlucci and held the gun to his head.

Carlucci opened his eyes very slowly and they almost popped out of his head when he saw Brian.

"Wa', wha'appened?" he said in a strangled whisper. "Now," replied Brian in an icy voice, "You can tell me what I want to know. Who set me up? Don't waste my time telling lies. Come on, talk!" He rammed the gun into Carlucci's neck.

Carlucci quivered as he stammered in reply, "Ah 'ad orders from Mr. Slovak to take out ya and Garforth. Ah was going to be paid 10,000 pounds."

Brian had the second recovered dart in the tube between his fingers like a cigarette. Without any feeling at all he put it casually to his lips and blew. Carlucci slumped down, dead. The poison was good enough for double duty, Brian found out.

Looking around the luxurious house, Brian gathered up all his things. On the table were his wallet and van keys. That made him think, so he emptied all the wallets of the boys. They would not be needing them again anyway where they were going. His wallet had false papers, but his fingerprints might be around. He couldn't risk that. They had taken his gloves off when they captured him. Now he tried to wipe off everywhere he had touched, including the chair and the bed. He again retrieved the two darts and flushed them and the tubes down the toilet.

He came out of Garforth's house cautiously. It was raining and there was no one about at that time of morning. He crossed the road without anyone seeing him. He had checked the time as being about 4:20 a.m. He had his suitcase with him, so he decided to go right away to his own apartment. He went to get his van, but it was gone. Likely, someone had seen him being marched into the Garforth house and figured he wasn't coming back and had stolen the van.

He started walking up the street. When he saw a car approach, he ducked out of sight. After a painful hike of about twenty minutes, he came out on the A13 and stood until a late taxi showed. He gave the guy two pounds to take him to the subway, which was right around the corner, but he didn't know that and was ridden for about two miles.

He rode the subway to his house. He had a key hidden and was soon able to get a good shower and get to bed. He ached all over his body, which seemed to be covered with black bruises, but he didn't seem to have any broken bones. He had a splitting headache too, but he was glad to be alive.

The alarm clock when off at nine o'clock. He had set it so he could talk to Mr. Slovak as soon as possible. Getting dressed took him a long time because he was so sore. Slowly he went out to a public box to make his call. He got through right away to The Organization and made arrangements to talk to Mr. Slovak at one p.m., the earliest possible time.

Coming back to the phone at one, he spoke to Mr. Slovak, "I'm awfully sorry, but there was a bad mix-up. I was captured and never did get the chance to let Carlucci know who I was. We were never alone." He had thought things out and decided that he would have to get Slovak before Slovak got him. He had no idea where Slovak lived and he didn't want to take him out too directly. He had no way of knowing how The Organization would take it, or even if Slovak was working on orders from them. But he did figure that Slovak would need some time to set him up again. In the meantime, forewarned was forearmed, and he had to beat him to the punch or die trying.

The next day they met at Mary's house. Slovak, Mr. Ante, and Brian. Mr. Ante was upset when he saw all the bruises, as was Mary and of course, Slovak. They wanted all details. Brian told them as much as he wanted them to know with no mention of the set-up.

Brian paid careful attention to how Mary reacted to his description of his experience at the hands of the Garforth mob. He thought he saw several knowing glances pass between her and Slovak. She, too, was in on the plot to remove him, he felt.

"I was grabbed by these three guys and they had a good look at me and Carlucci knew me. Then I got lucky and was able to take them all out."

Mr. Ante said, "All's well that ends well I guess. You are a lucky man. Go away and have a good rest. You did a good job as usual, right Slovak?"

As sore as Brian felt, he started immediately to look for another apartment. He really liked the one he had, but Slovak could very easily send someone round, and he wasn't about to take that chance. He quickly got another nice place with a shielded entrance in a mews. When money didn't matter, it made a world of difference. But he still used the old place for his mail. He never came for it at the same time any day and he never stayed more than a few minutes at a time.

Now he began his plans to take out Slovak. He knew he would not be safe as long as Slovak was alive.

Chapter 31

Shortly after the first of the year, Brian went in search of a house of his own. Mr. Ante had often said that a person in their line of work was better off if he had a second place—"a bolt hole" as it was—a place to hide for a few days, and one that he could get to quickly, without a lot of trouble.

It took awhile, but he finally came up with what he wanted. It was on Clancy Street off King's Cross Road, and there was a double-car garage. The last time he had hired a van it had stalled twice and he couldn't afford to take risks like that. With his own garage, he could buy his own van, which he did. He had to scout around until he got what he wanted, a half-ton in good shape. He overhauled it and put on new tires. He bought some tradesmen's logos, the kind you stick on the sides, and one of Grace's male friends furnished him with license plates.

When Brian returned from the race track one day, his landlady told him that the police were looking for him. He was to report right away to the station. It was urgent. "What the hell do they want with me?" he thought. He knew a moment of panic, then, "If they knew anything, they would be here waiting." He headed down to the station right away.

At the station, he told the desk sergeant who he was and was asked to sit down. He was on tenterhooks.

The inspector came in and looked at him. "Are you Mr. Brian Tilson from Beeston in Leeds, Yorkshire?" he asked in a very solemn voice.

Brian looked at him with a sinking feeling. "Yes," he replied in a low voice.

"Mr. Tilson," said the inspector, "we have received a phone message from Leeds City Police asking us to find you. It's been a long job, but we have to inform you there has been an awful accident at your father's house, a fire. I'm afraid I have to tell you that your father and mother did not survive. I'm awfully sorry. If there is anything we can do to help you, please let us know." Brian thanked everyone for their kindness and hurried back to the apartment.

He called Annie in Germany right away. She said she would catch a plane as soon as possible. He wired her some money figuring she wouldn't have much for fare. Then he got out the car and started north.

His mother's sister had already started funeral arrangements. When Annie arrived, they attended to the hundreds of details together. As he stood at graveside, he had mixed feelings. Was this just another passing episode in life? The last two days didn't seem real to him. Brian felt all mix-ed up, but already he felt guilty for not keeping better watch on his mother and father.

Then in a flashback, he thought of Smoky Gibbs lying out there with the rain on his face, of Bob Dewhirst, and Pat Phillips. The utter waste of their lives.

His heart ached. Anger and frustration rose up in him. He had no one to talk with, to ease his pain. He tried to drown his sorrow, but getting drunk didn't help, it only made him feel worse.

And to make matters even worse, the investigation found that the short had occured in the electric blanket he had given his parents as a luxury. Brian felt like hell.

Chapter 32

Brian was working on getting a sun tan while he sat on a bench in the park. It was a slow process but he enjoyed relaxing and watching the kids at their play.

Late in the afternoon he called at his other apartment to collect his letters and found one there from Mr. Ante. It requested him to call to set up a special meeting to go over the Garforth job. He had not had any action for a month. Of course he received his check every two weeks, so The Organization was staying in touch with him all the time.

Since the Garforth job, he stayed at his newest apartment where he felt much safer, going to his other apartment at diferent times just to pick up his letters. He wasn't about to be caught napping if he could help it.

He stopped at a call box to get the place and time of the next meeting. He was given an address at High Holborn for the following day at one o'clock.

Arriving early, he parked across the road and sat in his car hoping to see the car that Mr. Slovak arrived in so he could get the license number and model. But Slovak came in a cab as did Mr. Ante. Brian parked in a parking lot down the road and walked a block back to the building.

He greeted both Mr. Ante and Mr. Slovak warmly and they in turn were cheerful. Mr. Ante gave him an envelope containing all the information he needed. It was an assignment for Philadelphia to take care of a corrupt politician. He was to leave in three weeks. Mr. Ante told him there would be another job after that one in America, to get rid of a drug dealer in Florida. But he was in South America and The Organization was waiting for him to get back before sending Brian after him.

Brian liked the idea of returning to the United States.

They went over again what happened on the Garforth job. Mr. Slovak seemed to be fishing to see if Brian had any inkling as to a Carlucci connection outside The Organization's business. After thinking things over later, he didn't feel he had given anything away.

Thinking along further, Brian was still looking for somewhere to start in his plan to take out Mr. Slovak. He couldn't go to Mr. Ante with his suspicions as he had nothing really to back them up—nothing positive. And he didn't know just how important Mr. Slovak was in the overall scheme of The Organization, so he had to be very careful.

Then a thought struck him, and brought him up with a terrific jolt. What if this was an Organization job? It could be. There was nothing that pointed to it being so, but at the same time there was nothing that said it wasn't. And how could he check it out to see? If he made a slight misstep, who would know where it could lead? Perhaps to the end of everything. For him anyway.

He was almost giving himself a headache trying to fathom the best thing to do. He had no one to talk it over with. He was just going around in circles and getting more worried the more he thought of it all. The only link he thought he could see was Mary Pearson, so he decided to see what he could do by placing her house under surveillance. He could just wait to see how things turned out. He had no plans at the present time as what else to do.

He hired an old car, and parked where he could watch her house without attracting too much attention. He wore an old hat and old clothes and made sure he didn't look too clean. He half expected someone to call the police and complain, but nobody did.

Mary lived a busy life and had a number of male friends. She was out most nights and didn't return until the wee hours—some nights not at all.

Then Brian's perseverance finally paid off after nine straight nights. He was bored and fed up to the teeth (really thinking he was backing a loser and almost ready to quit) when, just before dark, a gray BMW came up the street. It drove to a parking spot further down, and out stepped Mr. Slovak. Bingo.

As soon as Slovak entered Mary's house, Brian wrote down the license number and drove away. He headed right for the

"Angel" and some much-needed refreshments.

The next day early he went to a friend of Gracie's who owned a car dealership and asked how he could trace a car he wished to buy. The dealer told him to go to Somerset House, where every license in the British Isles is recorded. He drove there right away to make his inquiries.

Having the number and make, he had no problem. Within a few minutes he had all the information he needed. The car was registered to a Mr. Joseph Bowden, with an address of 82 Kenworthy Court, Kensington, just a short distance from Hyde Park. It was a very exclusive neighbourhood. Number 82 was in a series of brownstones and had a gate at the end of the court.

He parked at the entrance to the main road and resumed waiting (at which he was getting plenty of practice but not enjoying it one bit). After sitting for hours, he saw the BMW pass him and enter the court. He was out of the car in a flash and running to where the BMW parked. He saw Mr. Slovak get out of the car and enter 82. Ha! He felt real good.

Mr. Slovak had not garaged the car, which meant that he would be going out again. Brian decided to wait some more and see what happened. He then moved his car to be facing out to the main road, ready to follow Mr. Slovak if possible.

About an hour later, after dark, he saw the car pull out with only Slovak in it.

Following close behind, he went about three blocks before he saw the BMW pull into the pub parking lot. Slovak parked and went in. "Now what to do?" Brian asked himself. He had a perfect chance here, with the parking lot not too well-lit and the BMW off to one side. But he could not use a noose or his favourite darts. They would be a sure giveaway to The Organization. He had to use some other method. The cruder the better so that it would not look like a planned job.

Opening the trunk of the hired car, he checked and found it empty—not even a jack handle. But, after striking a match, he pulled out a piece of carpet and there was an old rusty screw driver—just the thing.

Going over to the BMW he found it wasn't locked so he climbed in the back to wait. He had the far door open a little so that if Slovak brought anyone with him he could slide out and slip away. After what seemed years, he saw Slovak come out through the door alone and walk towards his car. He opened the driver's door, then pulled it shut with a slam. There was no one else in sight. Slovak then reached forward and inserted the key in the ignition. As he did so, Brian pushed his head forward as hard as he could, then struck downward with the screw driver into his back with as much force as he could muster, again and again. Slovak never knew what hit him. He let out just one, "Ha."

Brian went through his pockets, tearing them and removing everything including his watch to make it look like a frenzied robbery. He had no fear of fingerprints as he wore his gloves. He looked around carefully and seeing nothing, walked to his own car, which he had left in an adjoining lot. He had taken care of his mortal enemy. But—and it was a big but—he still didn't know if Slovak was acting alone or for The Organization.

Chapter 33

Waking early, Brian stretched and looked around his luxurious apartment. He smiled smugly. "Hey," he thought, "I've got it made. And this is what is what it is going to be like from now on." He got out of bed, had a lazy shower and good breakfast, then slumped on the sofa and wondered what to do with himself.

He hadn't heard from his sister, Annie, since the funeral. She seemed okay then. He dialed her number right away. She sounded upset. Bill was having a hard time keeping a job and things were going downhill fast.

On the spur of the moment he decided to go see her right away. Calling Gatwick, he found a plane was leaving in an hour—time for him to make it if he hurried.

Three hours later he walked into her apartment. She, the children and Bill were overjoyed to see him. It took some time to settle down.

They had refused time after time to take money from him, saying they were doing all right. Now he could see it was just pride that made them say so.

After talking for awhile, he saw they were at a dead-end, and did some fast thinking. He asked them straight out, "Will you come back to England with me? I have seen a wonderful little house for rent and I am thinking to borrow some money and get into my own business. As I travel a lot, I need a partner."

Annie looked at him, "Our Brian. If ya want Bill to help ya, we would love to do it. I'm afraid there isn't much for us here. We would be better off at home." They quickly disposed of the few things they had, packed their clothes, and caught a plane to Gatwick.

Bill Feeney, Annie's husband, had been a promising footballer until a knee injury put an end to that. But he was a good cabinet maker. They stayed the night at an hotel at Gatwick and the next morning Brian got his car. Starting out an easy pace, they got onto the M4 and headed for Newbury in Wiltshire. On one of his trips into the countryside, Brian saw a lovely house for rent and thought they could use it for a base as they explored the section.

If they didn't find what they wanted there, they could move on. This suited Bill and Annie. They still hadn't realized how their luck had changed so dramatically. Brian was trying hard not to tell them what to do. Bill was easy-going and he knew he would have to do what Brian planned.

Everyone liked the house. After looking up the real estate agent, they rented it. Since it was furnished, they were able to move in right away.

Two days later, Bill and Brian toured with the local real estate agents again—this time to find a business. With quite a few from which to choose, they came to Stockcross. Bill saw a house with a workshop in the rear and was instantly taken with it. "Ee luck at this! I knaw arh Annie el love this place. Let's go an bring 'er!" Brian put down a deposit. He didn't want to risk losing it after seeing Bill's reaction and he liked it too. An older, four bedroom house with two stories, it had two acres with lovely trees, stables and a full workshop in the rear. 62 Apple Lane, Shortcross, was beautiful.

Jack Grace had been the village joiner for many years, but wanted to retire, so he was willing to make a quick deal. Brian made a big pretense out of completing mortgage forms and payment paper. He didn't want them to be asking questions about where the money came from.

As soon as he returned to London, he arranged to pay everything off. He established trust funds for the children, Annie, and Bill.

Chapter 34

Brian stayed at the Rutland House in Philadelphia for two weeks while his whiskers grew. He had a phobia about being clean-shaven while he was on the job. People took him for older when he had a beard. That was one of his assets. As a young-looking person, most people didn't remember him. He fit in anywhere he was and made every effort to remain unseen.

He donned a false beard in the public restroom as soon as he left the plane. Not shaving was a ticklish business, but he had long ago decided to grow the real thing as needed.

He spent a lot of time studying his orders, which concerned a prominent politician who apparently had taken one too many payoffs and hadn't delivered what he had promised. He challenged his foes to do their worst, apparently figuring he was too important for them to do anything about it. Dr. Frances Kelly was a third generation Irishman, a loud mouth, six-foot-two, and two-hundred-twenty pounds. He had played football in college and started out as a dentist, becoming quite successful. And then, like a lot of Irishmen, he had gravitated into politics. Before long he was for sale to the highest bidder.

With his growing affluence, he moved out of the city that spawned him, with his wife and two sons, and bought a lovely ten-acre property at Newton, a better-class small town within easy reach of the city.

Brian was much impressed by the large, beautiful Tudor-style house with it's swimming pool in the rear. He saw the possibilities of the rough uneven, rising ground in the back of the house as being an advantage to him.

As he surveyed the place, he mused that being for sale really paid off. A crooked politician without a conscience could make a fortune until he became too greedy, reached too far, or stepped on too many toes. This Dr. Kelly obviously had done.

Brian oriented himself with a local map. He left his rented car about a mile back from the property. He wore rough clothes for walking the briars and brush to the top of the rise. From there he could look down into the back yard and see everything.

It was Friday. No one was home so he went down as far as he could and discovered he could get within fifteen feet of the edge of the water without being seen. There was a six-foot concrete walk around the pool.

With plenty of cover, the dart would be the ideal method. No noise, no mess and he knew from his previous experiences he could be long gone before people knew what caused the trouble.

The next day, Brian waited from two o'clock until dark, but Kelly did not show. He was back waiting at one o'clock Sunday. Lots of young people were there, sunning and enjoying themselves all day long.

About four o'clock the kids started to leave and older people came out. Kelly was among them. He wore swimming trunks and was talking to an aide as he came toward the pool. "I know you can do it, Tom," he said, just before he dove in and came up spouting water.

He swam across the pool, climbed out and stood six feet in front of Brian for a moment as he shook off the water and prepared to dive in again. Brian had his dart ready. Now he blew it right between his broad shoulders just as Kelly started his dive. Brian immediately started up the slope to make his escape.

After the long hike back to his car, he was putting his key in the lock when two young men approached and said, "Hi, Mac. Can we catch a ride to the end of the road? We are tired of walking." Brian couldn't very well refuse. He always tried to be agreeable so that people wouldn't remember him. The smaller one climbed into the back seat and promptly pulled a bottle from a knapsack. He took a good swig and handed the bottle to his buddy, who in turn had a pull. He offered the bottle to Brian, "Would you care for a drink?" he asked.

They had just reached an intersection. With the guy waving the bottle in his face, Brian was distracted, and as he was used to doing in England, he looked first right as he edged out into the intersection without stopping and never saw the little truck which slammed into him. The whiskey from the bottle spilled all over him.

Within minutes the police were there. The smell of whiskey didn't help Brian at all. The truck driver was yelling, "This damn fool pulled out right in front of me. I couldn't avoid him."

Brian was confused and shook up and the two guys didn't help. The police threw them all in the back of the patrol care when it seemed apparent they were all drunk, and bundled them off to jail.

As soon as Brian's head cleared, he began to think of his dart tubes. He had not been searched yet, but he knew he could be eventually, so he began to look for somewhere to dump them safely and not be seen. He stayed cool and waited his chance. He was ice cold and not worried.

Reaching the station house, they had to empty their pockets and were put in a temporary holding cell along with a bunch of other guys. The cell was almost full and the guys were sitting on the floor, so he moved over and sat down also on the floor near the foot of a small iron bed. He reached behind his back, putting both hands around the bottom of the leg of the bed nearest the wall. He lifted it ever so slightly and felt with his finger to see if it was hollow. It was. Pulling his feet up under him, he reached down to his sock (making sure no one was watching him). He took out the dart case, wrapped the cotton around the two remaining darts, and slipped them behind him. Lifting the bed leg again, very, very gently, he inserted the pack into the leg, praying all the time that he wouldn't touch the poisoned end. If he did, it wouldn't matter, he would never know! He heaved a long sigh of relief. He felt he was home safe.

When Brian was examined by a doctor and determined by a breath analyzer to be alcohol free, the authorities believed his story. He was summoned to appear in court the following week for careless driving.

The next day he had the first good shave in weeks. It felt good. He called the airport and booked a flight back to England for the following day. He wore the false beard until he reached the airport. He left his rental car in the hotel parking lot.

As soon as he reached home, he destroyed that set of identification papers. He wouldn't be needing them again.

Chapter 35

Pat Rowan sat his desk making our reports. For eighteen years, he had been with the Newton Police force, serving as a detective (a good one) for twelve of those. He could retire in another two years on full pension but intended to stay on as long as he was allowed to. He liked his job and his chief, Arthur Stacey. Stacey never pushed too much but liked to see results, and Pat tried hard to get them for him.

He had never cared for the paper work, but it had to be done, and it was the end of the month. He was staying a bit late this Sunday to finish clearing his desk. Besides, the air conditioning in the office felt good on such a hot day.

As the phone rang for the umpteenth time, he lifted the receiver to his ear and said in an even tone, "Newton Police, Rowan. Can I help you?" A very excited voice at the other end gabbled away. "Hold it. Hold it. Slow down! I can't understand a word you are saying," he said to cut off the young man on the other end of the phone. "Now just count to three and start again." As he spoke he reached for a paper pad and pencil and wrote the address given him.

It was the country home of Francis Kelly, well-known Philadelphia politician, out on Salem Road. He knew the place well as he had been there a few times.

Within fifteen minutes, he pulled up in front of the beautiful big house. George Day and Jack Dolan were in a second car right behind him. They had worked together for years and knew each other's ways.

Pat had already called the police photographer and the county mobile crime unit. It wouldn't be long before police were swarming all over the place. The front door was opened by an upset young man, about eighteen years old. He said in a choked voice, "I'm Jack Kelly. My dad is out back by the swimming pool. We pulled him out of the water and he is dead and we don't know how." He stood there looking like a lost soul.

Pat patted him on the shoulder and replied, "Will you take me to the pool, please. Just try and take it easy." He followed the young man through the crowded, silent house. There were young people all over the place, but you could hear a pin drop. Pat and his fellow officers came out through the sliding patio doors to the rear walk around the pool. Older people sat at numerous tables, speaking in low voices to each other.

The body was lying at the side of the pool with a bed sheet thrown over it. When Pat pulled back the corner over the face, he recognized Frank Kelly. He had seen his picture often enough in the papers and had seen him in town a couple of times. He couldn't seen any obvious cause of death so decided to wait for the medical examiner.

It looked like heart seizure, so he just asked a couple of questions and prepared to go home for his own long-awaited swim. He asked everyone to stay around for a little while longer.

Shortly, the medical examiner arrived. He was on his knees running his hands over the body, and called Pat over. "Pat, I don't like the look of this. I don't think this is a heart attack. He has all the signs of a seizure, but it could be poison. Stop everyone from leaving until we find out some things."

The first person he spoke to was Ed Cassidy, who had been Kelly's aide for years. He was the one who jumped into the pool and brought Kelly out, when he noticed he didn't surface from his dive.

Cassidy was very upset. Pat spoke gently to him. "Take your time and try to remember just what happened. Tell me what you can." Cassidy looked awful. He had a stiff drink to try to help him, but he was in a state of shock. His bushy hair was drying out and kept falling down across his full face. He was about thirty-five years old. At about six-foot-three and about two hundred pounds, he looked to be in good shape. He answered Pat in a quiet and girlish voice, but he looked anything but girlish.

"I was standing at the end of the pool when Dr. Kelly called me. I was talking to Mr. Varley when I turned and saw him sort of flop into the water. He was a fair swimmer and it was unusual to see him go in like that. So I watched him, and when he didn't make any movement, right away I knew something was wrong. I went in to bring him out. I guess I yelled for the others to help. We pulled him out onto the side and I tried mouth-to-mouth resuscitation but there was no response, so somebody called you. It was all so sudden..." He paused.

Pat talked to about twenty people and everybody had the same story. Nobody had been closer than at least twenty feet to Kelly. He asked Cassidy to go and stand where he had seen his boss stand, then to topple in the water the same way he had seen Kelly do. Cassidy did this a number of times.

After Pat had taken all the statements, he went home. He couldn't do any more until he knew the cause of death. Kelly had no history of heart trouble, and recently had been to his doctor and had received a clean bill of health.

As he walked from his car in the parking lot on Monday morning, Chief Stacey waited for him saying, "Seems like Big Mouth Kelly got his. Got any ideas? It sure is no loss anyway." They walked together down the building corridor.

Pat continued on his routine duties through the day. At three p.m., Molly, the dispatcher, rang his desk saying, "Medical examiner on line 2."

Jim Gallagher, who was new to his job, tended to get excited easily. His office and the county mortuary were in Media, about twenty miles away.

"Pat," he answered, excitedly, "We have a murder on our hands. Come on down as quick as you can!"

Gallagher, who was waiting impatiently for him, led him down to the cutting room. On a table was Kelly's body. "I came in early but couldn't get to the autopsy right away. I really had a hell of a time finding out what did the damage. As I suspected, it was poison. Look at this." He turned Kelly over on his face. Near his right shoulder blade was a large pimple with a pin prick in the center. A small metal tray near the table held the tiny metal dart. "This is what I took from the body," he said, handing it to Pat.

"I went over the body three times before I found it," he said. "I have heard of these things. They are like South American curare darts, but are more deadly and quicker-acting. If he had been dressed, the dart could have been pulled out by his clothing when he was moved, and we never have seen it or known what it did." He shook his head, "You have a tough job with this one. I don't envy you one bit."

Pat had pictures taken of the body and the dart, then returned to the office. When Cassidy reenacted the way Kelly had gone in the water, Pat had the police photographer take a video and plenty of still pictures of the action. Now he sat in the office looking them over. At the time, he had all the people there take up the positions they were in when Kelly died.

Looking at the video, he saw that no one could have been near enough to shoot the dart without being seen. Everything was so open. People were moving about all the time.

The next morning he returned to the house with his good buddy George Day. George had been with the department for four years and was smart and full of enthusiasm. He always had a joke and was a good man to have around. He had been a patrolman with the Philadelphia City Police and waited a long time for an opening with the Newtown Police. At six-foot-six and two-hundred-twenty pounds, Day was a valuable addition to the staff.

The two men started at the edge of the swimming pool, combing every inch of the ground. With their backs to where Kelly had fallen, they worked up to the rough ground. Starting up the incline at the top of the low wall, they coursed back and forth among the rough brush.

It was George who found a number of small depressions. "Over here, Pat," he called, pointing to the marks made by someone's heels on the ground, and a slight depression where the person must have sat.

Pat crouched down and saw that the distance was about right to the pool and an assailant would be hidden by the underbrush, almost invisible from the house. The marks going up the hill made it plain that someone had walked up and down the steep incline.

They worked their way up the slope, not without difficulty, until they reached the top. Turning around, they say they had a good view of the entire property. They continued to follow the faint trail, winding back and forth until they came out on the road parallel to the Kelly property. The trail ended there.

Retracing their steps slowly and carefully, they searched the ground for anything at all, and near the top of the hill, their perseverance paid off. Kicking around in a pile of leaves, George spotted some color and retrieved a crumpled piece of paper. Dropping it into an envelope, he gave a grunt of satisfaction.

"What do you say we call it enough for now," he said. "I don't think it will do any good to search any more. This guy was very careful. He must have been here a number of times judging by the trail he made. If he had only come once, we would have had a much worse time following him, but he made quite a trail. With the ground hard, there isn't a single foot print. This was planned for a while."

Returning to the offices, they gave the piece of paper to the fingerprint department to see if they could find anything. It was a slim chance, but the only one they had. Nothing. After checking their notes, they decided that the next day they would check along Madison Road where the trail ended. There were no houses within half a mile of the spot they marked, but they decided to stop every car that came along to ask if anyone remembered seeing a parked car or anything else unusual on Sunday.

They had been there all day and stopped about twenty cars. They were ready to quit when they struck gold. A young high school guy and his girl had seen a Chevy parked there the last two Sundays. It was a blue, 1986 with a long scrape on the left side. Between them, they were able to remember the last two numbers on the license plate.

After talking together some more, the kids remembered there was an advertisement for a leasing outfit in Philadelphia on the door panel.

Wednesday morning at the station, Pat and his investigating team reviewed what they had. With the last two numbers on the license plate and the name of the leasing company, the agency, with the help of the computer was able to identify its car.

The car had been leased to a Mr. Timothy Walker who was staying at Rutland House in Philadelphia.

As they waited for another call, Molly came in the office and passed a paper to Pat. "I heard you talking about a blue Chevy and it sort of rung a bell, but it took me some time to put things together. This car was in an accident at Madison Road on Sunday and the driver was put in the cells. He was covered with whiskey, but when the doctor checked him he was sober. No alcohol in his body. When he cleared himself, he was released and is due in court next week. Here is a copy of his summons.

"They had the killer in the cells on Sunday and didn't know

it," said Pat.

Getting out the car, they raced down to the Rutland only to find that Mr. Walker had checked out Monday morning and left for the airport. The Chevy was sitting there in the parking lot. After being checked for fingerprints, it was released to the agency. It had been wiped clean—not even a smudge inside. A check at the airport confirmed at a Mr. Walker had left on a flight for London on Monday. Pat and George were left with nothing.

Chapter 36

Brian's next directions were to proceed to Miami, Florida, then on to Tampa to deal with a Mr. Ralph Kirchoff who was a wealthy landowner and yachtsman. He traveled all over South America and was reputed to be involved in every crooked deal in Florida. However, nothing had been proven. And because of his connections, the police were powerless.

When he reached Miami the next day, he rented a car and drove around to check an address he had been given to use if he needed materials or help. It turned out to be a nice little sporting goods store. He walked in and purchased a pair of sun glasses and a map of the West Coast without attempting to make further contact. He just looked the guy over before he left.

Waking early the next morning, he still felt jet lag, but figured it would clear off after a few days. In the meantime, he would just take it easy. He checked his map and drove across the state on Alligator Alley. He wanted to connect with US 41 in Naples. US 41, better known as the Tamiami Trail, is a direct road up the West Coast to Tampa. Brian enjoyed the drive, the sunshine and the scenery, which was unusual to him.

Passing through Fort Myers, Punta Gorda, Venice and Sarasota, Brian realized he was nearing his destination. He pulled off to the side, read his map and saw that he could turn off at Route 60 and go right out to the bay. Kirchoff's house was on North Melrose, so Brian found a nice motel on Brookwood Drive, just a few blocks from there.

As usual, he was again growing his whiskers. He had grown a beard so many times that now he was almost used to it.

He walked around the neighbourhood and spotted Kirchoff's house surrounded by palm trees, with its own private dock.

He sat on a nearby bench, did some sketching and some measuring as best he could by eye of distances, writing everything down. He also watched to see if he could spot Kirchoff, but with no luck.

The second day, Brian walked toward the dock and met a young, gangly fellow of about fourteen, with a pimply face, who was doing some fishing. "Hi, how's it going. Are you catching anything," Brian asked him.

He quizzed the boy and asked him who owned the yacht. The kid said, "Oh that's Mr. Kirchoff's. They will be leaving in about an hour. He has another house in Sarasota and won't be back for at least a month. I know because my brother works for him on the boat and I will be going down there a few days next week. It's a lot better place than this—closer to the beach—on Lincoln Drive." That was just what Brian needed, since the Tampa address was the only one he had for Kirchoff.

The kid kept babbling, but Brian cut him short and returned to the motel. He got out his maps again and found that Lincoln Drive was not too far from Route 41, so he packed his bags and drove to Sarasota, checking into a motel near the beach. The next day, he walked the district. This Kirchoff house had a wire fence all around it. It was a single-story house with a sizable area for tables set out between the house and the wooden dock.

When he went by the house the first time, the boat hadn't arrived. Looking things over very intently, he was trying to set something up, but he had to wait until the yacht arrived the next morning.

When it docked, he saw three people on the deck, and he recognized Kirchoff from his large, thick body and mane of white hair. He walked very straight and stiff which he learned from his years in the navy, according to Brian's information sheet. He was easy to identify.

There seemed to be a party going every night. The bright lights were on and sometimes he heard a band playing. There were always a number of people milling around between the dock and the house.

After watching for a few nights, Brian decided that he would take a long shot. He just could not get up close enough. He didn't like long distance work because it was less accurate.

He returned to Miami and called the sports shop. His contact told him to call back in an hour for information on where to pick up his order. At that address he acquired a Winchester 303 with a silencer and telescopic scopes. He returned to Sarasota, satisfied with his purchases.

While in Miami, he spoke with Mr. Ante, and was told to call him again later. He bought a couple hundred feet of black nylon rope. Across the street from Kirchoff's dock was a single story house with a pitched roof. Over the roof, he could see a chimney. He figured that the distance from a certain spot on the roof to his target area would be about three hundred feet, well within the range of his Winchester. He figured he could do the job from up there, and he knew how he would get to the top of the roof.

He would lie on the roof, his feet against the chimney and shoot over the ridge of the house. Dressed in his darkest clothes, he left the car near the garage of the house he selected as soon as it was dark. Luckily there didn't appear to be anyone home as he walked to the front yard and passed his rope around a tree. He fastened the two ends together and tied them to a piece of stick. He flung the stick over the house top, then walked around to the back. but the stick was not down far enough for him to reach so he walked back again to the front, retrieved his rope and threw it over again, this time giving an extra heave. It was successful.

He slung the rifle over his back and easily climbed the wall and the roof, up as far as the chimney. He took great care not to make any noise or disturb anyone. As he surmised, the chimney was about four feet from the peak of the roof.

When he looked over the peak, he had a clear view. The tree in the front yard was off to his left. He was just at the edge of its branches and had an uninterrupted view of the entire right yard and deck of the yard. That had been his big worry--that the tree would block his vision.

Festivities had already started for the night. A good crowd was milling around with drinks and the band was blaring loudly. Brian could see a number of guards all around at different places. Kirchoff was not in sight yet, so Brian settled down to wait. He was satisfied that he could not be seen and began making a few preparations

He straightened out the rope so he could make a quick descent. He straightened the wire coat hanger he brought to fasten to the gun before he dropped it down to dangle inside the chimney. Finally, he adjusted the sights again and began to wait for Kirchoff.

Twenty minutes later, Kirchoff appeared at the rear of the house and walked toward the deck of the yacht. He strolled around awhile then moved toward the target area. Brain had him lined up for a long time, but waited until he came to exactly where he wanted him for an almost sure shot. Kirchoff walked right to the spot and stopped to speak to a man. He was facing full front. Brian squeezed the trigger, and Kirchoff keeled over, dead before he reached the ground. Brian reached for his wire, fastened it to the gun, and flung the gun inside the chimney. Quickly he rappelled to the ground and wound up his rope as he walked to his car. He threw the coil into the rear seat as he opened the door, sat down in the driver's seat and started the engine. Coolly, he switched on his lights, and drove away.

During his morning walk, he felt good when he bought a newspaper and saw that Mr. Ralph Kirchoff had been shot to death the night before. The world was free of another drug dealer. Another drug-related gang slaying, said the paper. No arrests had been made yet.

He waited a few days before contacting Mr. Ante and returning to London. He could put up with this pace for a few days longer without any trouble. He enjoyed the sunshine.

Chapter 37

While Brian was in Miami to get the rifle for his last assignment, he had received a message to call Mr. Ante at a pre-arranged time in England. He called from a public telephone and was given a message in code which he had deciphered later at the motel. They didn't take any chances that someone could listen in on or intercept the messages. It was a slow, cumbersome way way of doing business, but had proved safe on a number of occasions.

The message said that his first orders had been countermanded. Instead of immediately returning to England, he would be required to stay in the U.S. another three weeks, at least, because he was likely to receive another assignment there. He was told to travel around as a tourist and have a good holiday at The Organization's expense. He was to call Mr. Ante at a prearranged time in two weeks.

Brian decided to go further north, near Tampa, away from where he had stayed before. On Hillsborough Avenue, near the Rogers Park golf course, he found a large motel with a nice swimming pool. He made up his mind to learn to play golf to help pass the idle hours. He still had his books and he studied and checked his speech daily. But he was tired of just sitting around studying.

Between his golf lessons, lounging on the beach and swimming, he did not have much time for anything else, but he did manage an enjoyable six-hour boat ride. His days passed quickly.

He called Mr. Ante at the appointed time, received his detailed instructions and spent a couple of hours deciphering them.

A Mr. George McCrone, who had absconded with funds from Northern Ireland, was believed to be in the Sarasota area. He was to be found and taken care of. He was highly dangerous, ruthless, strong, and surrounded by diehard "Pros." He already had a reputation as a cold-blooded killer, especially of Catholics, whom he hated with a passion. Brian was to be very careful.

He had been frequenting a night spot on the avenue and talked with some of the boys. He asked them, "Where is the action in Sarasota? Any good Irish spots there? I am moving down there and want some fun."

One recommended a motel on Bee Ridge Road. "It's close to the action. The guy knows how to keep his mouth shut and mind his own business." He looked at Brian knowingly and said, "Get a place at the back—it is quiet and you can get out in a hurry if you have to. Know what I mean? Keep mobile."

Losing no time, Brian moved next day getting a room at the back as advised. He could see the back route very easily and it looked well-used. He asked about the night spots and was told there were enough to suit all tastes.

He found the Hog's Head bar, about five minutes away from the motel, and began to make a few inquiries—as discreetly as possible. The first night he was there he had spotted a young fellow with a Belfast accent. Brian picked him out easily since he had heard it often enough on his tours of duty there. Brian had heard him speaking to two other Irishmen and had tried to manoeuvre round to speak to them. It took three nights to do so without appearing to be too eager or pushy. Finally he found himself sitting near the young Irishman. "Hi," he said to the guy. "Will you have a drink with me? It is so good to hear an English voice."

The kid was about twenty-one years old, but with the look of a city-raised kid. He looked Brian up and down and answered, "Well, what have we here? A Limey fresh out?"

Brian answered with a smile, "No, I'm just here for awhile and missing my good beer. It's nice to talk to someone who speaks English—it does get wearing listening to these Americans."

The guy looked back at Brian, "Aye, you'll get used to it after awhile. I haven't been here long myself, but, like you say, it does become mortifying." Then he reached out to shake hands. "I'm Tim Stewart."

They had a few drinks together and were getting along pretty good when two more Belfast men came to join them. Brian was introduced to Douglas Cronin and Stan—no surname, just Stan. He was a slender-built man about twenty-eight. Douglas was about thirty, with sandy hair and thin features. Both of them looked like they needed a good feed. Brian told them his name was George Nutt. He didn't think they would inquire further. When it got a bit late, he excused himself to leave.

Douglas said, as he rose to go, "See you tomorrow night, George, same place, same time. Eh, old man?"

Brian quickly agreed.

Going over the conversation he had with Stewart later on, he couldn't see if he had made any headway. He was working in the dark. He had let them know he worked with the RUC in Belfast and was all for the Pros in the Irish Question (he had discovered which side Doug was on). Brian thought he was possibly on to something because of the knowing glances that passed between the other men. Still, only time would tell. He felt he might as well see what he could get out of this connection anyway. He had nothing else to go on.

On Thursday night, Stewart had too much to drink and was sounding off on the Irish question. One of the other guys tried soothing him down, but the talk got hot about where the blame lay for "the troubles."

Brian tried to steer a middle course, never forgetting his mission—and to stay sober at all times, which was difficult. The beer was flowing and he had to refuse the offers several times. Then he heard what he had been waiting for. The name of McCrone was mentioned. He really paid attention.

But it was only mentioned in passing. McCrone was due in on Saturday, nothing further. After awhile the crowd dispersed.

Friday night was almost a repeat of Thursday except Stewart stayed sober. Doug and Stan were talking about going fishing on Saturday. "You will be welcome to come with us tomorrow if you like. Don't bother to bring anything except some beer—we have all the tackle," said Douglas. He gave Brian a time and place to meet them. "Don't be late. We leave before first light," said Stan.

When Brian arrived, Douglas, Stan, and another man, along with a another slightly-built guy who looked to be about thirty-years old were already on the dock. This guy had a mean look about him. He stood about five-ten and weighed roughly one-hundred-sixty pounds. He walked on the balls of his feet, lightly, like a prize fighter. His hair was brushed straight back and his sharp, sewer-rat eyes caused Brian to distrust him on sight.

They busied themselves getting the boat ready and it wasn't long before they had everything shipshape and ready to go. Then "the Weasel" (as Brian named him), the man who had been introduced as "Bill," said, "Well, as the other men didn't come, I'm going to cry off too. I'm going to take out the other boat and will meet you at the end of number six buoy in about five hours, if you have run up the flag for me, OK? That will be about twelve o'clock, agreed?"

Brian didn't know what they were talking about, but presumed that they had some arrangement for doing what they were doing. He intended to see what it was all about and go from there.

The three of them started out and ran for about an hour, not too fast, so they didn't cover much distance. The boys were talking about various things on the way out, when they stopped and put out their lines to fish. They brought out the beer, drank and stretched out. Stan said rather casually, "You know, George, the other night, you were asking about a Mr. McCrone, a George McCrone. I knew a fellow by that name—a big guy back in Belfast. Would that be him? Did you have anything in mind when you asked about him?" Brian was instantly on the alert. All his senses were jangling, but he answered lightly, "Well, to tell the truth, I was looking to get myself some easy money. In Tampa, I was told by some of the boys that a Mr. McCrone was looking for someone to do all kinds of different jobs and no questions asked. I could use some extra money. I wasn't about to ask any questions."

Stan asked more pointed questions and before long became abusive. Brian realized why he had been invited to take this fishing trip. They had somehow become suspicious. Brian tried his best to fend him off and finally in exasperation told him, "It seems to me you don't want to believe anything I say—so what? We don't have to live together. So as soon as I get off this boat, we separate and be gone. We can still be friends or not. It sure as hell doesn't matter to me. I don't want to fall out with anyone, OK?"

Douglas then stood up and went down into the tiny cabin, reappearing after a few minutes. He had a gun in his hand and pointed it in Brian's direction, "OK, whatever your name is, down into the cabin—now!"

Brian couldn't see what had gone wrong. He had tried to be very careful, but something had slipped somewhere. Douglas followed down to the cabin, and, after tying the tiller and slowing down the engine, Stan followed him.

Between them, they tied up Brian and dumped him on the floor. Then they went through his pockets and checked everything he had, which wasn't much. "You know McDermott said the other night he had seen this joker somewhere before. He thinks it was in Grady's bar in Belfast."

Brian remembered the barkeep looking twice at them the first time he walked into the bar—he was the victim of a once-in-a-lifetime coincidence! But he was sure at the time no one knew him except as a soldier in the army—so maybe he could bluff his way out yet. It remained to be seen.

Stan and Douglas, drinking more beer, questioned Brian. "What we want to know is. Why did you seek us out? And why the questions you asked?"

Then Douglas turned to Stan and said, "Why bother trying to get anything out of him? He is going to tell us a pack of lies anyway, unless I give him a good kicking."

They sat Brian up with his knees under his chin. They tied him this way because there wasn't much room in the tiny cabin. Doug aimed a kick right into his side with all his power. The breath flew out of Brian and he felt as if his ribs were broken. The pain was terrific. Another kick followed and another. Doug sat down on the bunk, blowing and all out of breath. "Well, you Limey bastard, are you going to say anything?" he asked. "I might as well tell you right now there will be no return trip for you—so to save yourself further grief, you may as well tell us what we want to know."

When Brian left that morning, he had put on double socks with his darts sewn into them. He was resting his left hand on the darts right now. Looking at Douglas, he thought, "Give me one chance you bastard, and your number is up."

Stan had tired of watching the beating, and stood up saying, "I am going to do some fishing until McCrone comes. Are you coming?" With that they both went up the small ladder to the deck.

This was the first Brian heard that McCrone was due. He was nauseated. He could hardly breathe with the pain in his ribs, but he started wriggling as soon as the men went up. He had a hell of a score to settle and he meant to settle it. Pulling and tugging, he felt a little give in the rope after awhile, but not enough to free his hands fully.

They had fastened his wrists, elbows and knees, then pulled his knees under his chin and fastened him there too. He could just get his hand up to his mouth, but he couldn't loosen anymore of the rope. He didn't know how much time he had before they would come back. Stretching as much as he could, he reached his darts and very carefully removed them from his sock. With sweat dripping from his eyes, he managed, after a long, painful struggle to wedge one tube under his chin in his jacket collar so he could reach it in a hurry. The ends were removed and it was near his mouth for action. Biting off the tip of the other one, he kept it in his mouth and waited. It was now or never.

It seemed like years. He could hear the two men as they discussed what they would do with their share of the money from the sale of the stuff McCrone was bringing for them to take ashore. From their conversation, it became apparent that the guy introduced as "Bill" was McCrone.

"You know we take all the risks and McCrone just brings it from the mother ship. We could take off with the stuff once we get it on board," said Stan. "Hey, why the hell don't we?" The reply from Douglas was somber, "Man, you come up with the most crazy schemes. He would cut us up into the smallest pieces and you know it. So don't be getting so brave all of a sudden. I'm going down to check on the Limey, and get another six-pack of beer."

Brian heard the footsteps on the deck as Douglas came towards the cabin. Brian steeled himself as the guy came down the small ladder and blocked out the light.

The cabin was not very high and Douglas had to stoop when he reached the bottom of the steps. When he put out his left hand to get the beer, Brian blew gently on the dart and it landed in Douglas's neck. It didn't travel more than six feet. Douglas just looked at Brian and crumpled to the deck, dead.

Brian could see a knife in Douglas's waistband, but he couldn't reach it. After a few minutes, Stan called down, "Hey, Doug, What's keeping you? Hurry up with that beer!" There was no answer, and, after waiting a short while, he came to the top of the steps and called again. Then he saw Doug's legs sticking out, and without thinking, he immediately jumped down the ladder, grabbed Douglas and turned him over, saying "What the bloody hell is going on?"

His eyes adjusted to the darkness and he saw Brian sitting there with what looked like a cigarette in his mouth. Then Brian spoke for the first time, hissing out the words, "Listen carefully, nit. If you touch your buddy, you will know he is dead. I killed him. I have a blow pipe aimed at your neck. Lie down on the deck right now or you are a dead man, too. Now!"

Stan threw himself flat. Brian told him, "Take out your knife very carefully. Very slowly inch it toward me. I can manage better without you, so don't try anything funny or brave, hear me?"

Stan did as he was told. It took Brian two minutes to get the knife and cut himself free. He was stiff and sore, but didn't dare rest.

He trussed Stan like a chicken, then sat down and had a sandwich and a beer, which made him feel better. He was going to be sore for quite awhile but he didn't think any ribs were broken.

Now he checked the time to see how long it would be before McCrone came with the cargo for them to take to the shore. He had not forgotten that McCrone mentioned a flag. He asked Stan about it. He had not threatened Stan since he first took charge. He needed him for awhile anyway and was careful how he handled him. He had taken loaded guns from Douglas and Stan.

Stan was trying to make a deal. He still didn't know that McCrone was the primary target. Now he offered to cut Brian in on the deal. "We are onto a good thing here," he said. "There are millions in it, and we are not greedy." When he saw he wasn't getting anywhere with that line, he switched to "the cause." "We are doing this for the cause in Northern Ireland. We have to get rid of those bastard Irish Catholics. It is not for us, but to get guns and things for the people back home, where I have a wife and two children."

Now Brian got really tough. He realized that McCrone would not approach the boat without the flag. It had to be some sort of a signal. "Well, you bastard, I wasn't in the British Army for nothing. They showed us how to obtain needed information, and now here goes." And he grabbed Stan between the legs and squeezed. Within seconds, Stan had told him all he wanted to know. Brian ran up an orange flag on the small mast.

As the meeting time neared, Brian went over a few things with Stan and learned additional information. A little twist here and there made him very talkative. The gang had an elaborate system of drug-smuggling going on and it made a good deal of money, all for themselves. Stan promised to cut Brian in.

Now as time was short, Brian tied Stan, with a fishing line, at the wheel. He secured his feet and knees to the top step. His hands were free. To anyone standing three yards away, he looked totally free. But a tight fishing line led from the steps to his fly and was fastened around his testicles. Only the two of them knew it was there. If Stan moved anywhere, he was in trouble. Brian put on Douglas' jersey and hat. He didn't expect to fool McCrone much, but he figured to get him close enough to get the drop on him, then wait to see how things turned out. From Stan's information, it appeared that McCrone's boat was larger and faster than theirs. If McCrone came close enough, he had to nail him as quickly as possible.

There weren't too many boats around. They had picked a place that would not be busy. The fishing thereabouts was not good.

At about 12:30, Stan, looking Gulfside, saw a boat traveling at a high speed. "This could be him," he said.

Brian told him in a grim voice, "For the last time I am telling you--if you so much as raise a finger, you are a dead duck, or at least a gelded one." He burst out laughing at Stan's expression.

Brian watched through the glasses to see if there was more than one man on board, but couldn't be sure. He could only see one. He would have to take the chance that McCrone was alone.

The speedboat came up fast, and for the last hundred yards, Brian ducked down below, standing where he could see Stan, and talking to him all the time to keep him under control. Brian knew a little about men and he knew he had Stan where he wanted him—in deadly fear of his life. He wasn't about to let him go.

As the other boat swung alongside, he popped out on deck. "Greetings to you, Mr. McCrone. As you can see, this gun is pointed right at your head, and I would have no hesitation pulling the trigger. Here, catch." He flung him the rope.

McCrone was so surprised, he fastened the rope. He couldn't really do anything else, having a gun in his face less than two yards away. But his sharp eyes were everywhere, looking for his chance. He didn't stay surprised for long, and Brian knew he had a tiger by the tail He was not about to underrate him or take chances. Without moving, he told McCrone to lie down on the deck. There was little movement of the boat. The wash had subsided and it was calm, with hardly any roll at all.

As McCrone started to go down on the deck, he suddenly threw himself at Brian, as hard as he could, in a rolling, desperate, last-ditch lunge. Brian, who was waiting for just such a move, skipped to the side and calmly shot McCrone right between the eyes. Using the other gun, without any hesitation, shot Stan through the heart and cut the fishing line which held him. He tumbled him down into the cabin, with McCrone after him and threw the guns down with them. He transferred some drug packets from the other boat. If they were ever found, it would look like a drug boat.

It took him about five minutes to check everything, to find the sea cocks and open them to flood the boat. She began to settle down fast. He closed the cabin door, so nothing would float away, and threw everything inside first.

Then he climbed into the other boat, restarted the motor and headed for the distant land—slowly at first until he saw that the first boat had disappeared beneath the surface. He stopped, and threw overboard all the bundles (presumably drugs) that were in the tiny cabin. He didn't want to be caught with them.

He had gone through the pockets of the dead men, removing identification and money. No use wasting it, he felt. With a cold beer in his hand, he was at peace with the world. He had no remorse about killing these three. He was getting used to it. He made his way to a landing without knowing where he was, and not caring. He ran slowly until he saw a much-used dock, pulled in and tied up among the other boats. Nobody noticed anything as he picked up his jacket and walked away.

Chapter 38

Ever since the Garforth deal, Brian had had an uneasy feeling. He could not shake the idea that he somehow had overstepped the mark with The Organization or that he had outlived his usefulness.

He knew full well that the present situation was too good to last for ever. He knew he had replaced someone and that someone would replace him. To that end, he had been thinking and planning as how he could escape from The Organization. It was not going to be easy.

Mr. Ante had casually mentioned that Mr. Slovak had returned to Germany and would have no further dealings with the firm—and that was all he had said.

Brian had lost the idealistic fervour that Mr.Ante had generated at first, with his call to rid the world of wrongdoers and to bring "justice" to bear. "Justice" was a word that Mr. Ante used often, and at first it had quite a ring.

Yes, he had quickly adjusted that fervour, feeling that he would be able to enrich himself while he carried out his idealism, and his ego bridged the gap. Now he was financially secure.

He discarded one plan after another before a workable one evolved. His line of thinking was to stay as close to his present living place as he could, figuring that The Organization would expect him to bolt as far away as possible.

On most of his assignments he had a full beard and long hair. He was sure that no one from The Organization, except Mr. Ante, had seen him at any time with this disguise or that he had ever been photographed that way. None of his passports showed him with a beard, either. He made sure by checking them.

He visited Grace. She gave him the name of John Moore—a forger, good photographer and printer of fake passports. He visited Moore, tell him he had made bad enemies and needed to make a move without leaving a trace.

For a while he had been looking for a man with his height and general build—with the idea of assuming his identity. On his last trip to Belfast, he had seen such a man. Len Healey was about five years older and fifteen pounds heavier, but Brian thought he would fit the bill. He wanted some small changes and he didn't have many options.

His inquiries showed that Healey had two sisters, both single, and he contrived to meet the twenty-year-old one. Mary was gabby, and, after he dated her a few times, he knew quite a lot about Len—all of which he wrote down for further study. He learned that Healey, under no circumstances would leave Northern Ireland. There was no danger of bumping into him elsewhere.

He took dozens of pictures of Len from different angles. This was difficult since he had to dream up all sorts of reasons to photograph a girlfriend's brother as well as find occasions when he could photograph Len without his knowing about it.

The time he spent on learning make-up came in handy. He had always kept his hair cut short on the back and sides, well-greased and neatly parted and his eyebrows were trimmed. Now with the help of Mr. Moore, he decided to leave his hair long and loose, brushed straight back, like Healey's. His eyebrows would be left to grow ragged, plugs placed in his nose to fill it out and his gums padded to fill out his jaws. The result was startling. He was more like Len Healey than Healey himself. He intended to use colored lenses but didn't let Moore know that. They juggled a number of different make-ups and took lots of pictures.

Brian had a good reason. He figured when he got the different passports, Mr. Moore would not be able to tell anyone which one he used—if he wanted to—and he could pick out at his leisure the one that suited him.

Before paying the man, he demanded all the pictures, because he knew full well that if anyone came round with the money, he would be sold out—there was no honour among thieves. None of the passports had a name or address. The less Mr. Moore knew, the better—but he was careful to "carelessly" drop the name Australia as the place he thought he might be safe in.

Chapter 39

Now that he had acquired a complete new identity—what he had to do was establish it. He removed all of the disguise before he returned to his apartment.

His first step was to call his friend Ernest Back (who he had met on several occasions in the park) and to get together with him. He told Ernest that another friend had asked him to look for a good investment in an apartment house. The two met and canvassed the immediate neighbourhood. They quickly narrowed the choice down to two houses and after looking at both twice, decided on one. It had two empty apartments, and this was one of the factors that made them agree on it. Ernest, they decided, would manage the house and would occupy the ground apartment. The house had always been handled by an absentee landlord before. The address was 25 Norton Street NW2.

There were six apartments in the building and the other empty one, on the second floor rear, was furnished. Brian checked out all the house—he could see an excellent escape route via a short drop from his window onto the next-door store's roof-top and easy access to the street, in case he every needed it.

Brian figured he could trust Mary Burns (his good friend from the "Angel") as much as anyone, so he went to see her at her apartment. He asked, "Would you do me a big favour? I have a friend who wants to rent an apartment. Will you please call the manager for me and make the arrangements?" He dialed the number of Ernest Back, and didn't let her see it—and so it was all arranged.

Two days later he arrived at the front door in his disguise, wearing his platform shoes which made him two inches taller.

This was the acid test. He felt if he could fool Ernest Back, he would be able to carry it off. Since Ernest had not known him a long time, he thought, if it fails and Ernest recognized him, he could pass it off as a joke. Then he would just return to the planning board. He spent all morning with the photos in front of him trying to make the disguise perfect. For weeks he had been using the Belfast accent every chance he got (around people who didn't know him). Now with his heart in his mouth, he knocked on the door of his own apartment house.

He need not have worried, Ernest made him very welcome. "Come on in. I expected you yesterday!" he said. "The vacant apartment is on the second floor. Come on, let's take a look at it right away." He looked at the slightly stooped man with curiosity. "Have you been in London very long?" he asked.

Brian replied, "I came about two weeks ago, and I have been staying with my sister in Islington. She doesn't have enough room for me." That sounded like a good excuse and explained why a woman had called to book the apartment. After checking it out, Brian approved it, took the keys and paid the rent.

He found that he was able to deceive Ernest without being scared. Now he was looking forward to the next step--for now the die had been cast.

For a while he intended to share his time between this new apartment and the other. He didn't want to disappear from Crabb Court—the present apartment—until Len Healey had become firmly established. So daily, he would leave Norton Street and travel by bus to where he had left his car—then travel to Crabb Court and spend the day.

The days were short, as darkness came early. He hoped no one would see him leave, so he set the TV with a timer to shut off at twelve o'clock. The lights would go off also. Then, a little at a time, he took out his clothes, most of which he discarded, keeping those items he sometimes wore when he was on jobs for The Organization. He had already bought a new wardrobe of clothes more loosely-fitting than those he had formerly worn, and he installed them at Norton Street. Now he bought all new furniture, including a new bed. It was one of the best. He had the money and now he was going to enjoy it.

He began to practice long and hard to slow down his walk, and he carried a stick to remind him. He wore a tight knee-bandage on his right knee to make him remember to walk slow, and he smiled often with satisfaction when he found himself just sauntering along with all the time in the world. But as always he stayed on the alert. He had only one life.

Brian had been living at Norton Street about three weeks when he decided that the time had come. He talked with Mr. Ante the week before and assured him that he was doing OK and would soon be able to resume his normal activities—but he had also told him that he thought he was being followed. Because Mr. Ante knew that Brian had incurred the wrath of the local pimps, he advised him to move out of that neighbourhood. Brian thought it was all now fitting together.

He left Norton Street that final morning and caught the bus down to Kings Cross, changing buses twice before he went to Crabb Court. He had sold the house on Clancy Street two days before and already collected his money. He thought, with a chuckle, "I will have to get a bank deposit box before it is stolen from me." He left the car at Crabb Court to confuse anyone who might be looking for him, since Mr. Ante knew about the car. He did not want to be traced.

Brian also stripped his other safe deposit boxes and put them into new banks. When The Organization started to check, his assets would be gone. At the same time he changed the letters he left with his solicitors; everything he possessed he tabulated and wrote down all the names and numbers as to where his money was hidden. Brian didn't want his sister Annie to miss one penny if he could help it.

The apartment at Norton Street was a large, airy place, and he enjoyed living there. It was further away from the park than the other one, but he started right away to take a walk every day. He checked every cross street so that in the event of having to move quickly, he would know the best means of exit.

He also checked out and later rented another small furnished apartment, at Hill Street, about a five-minute walk away and moved some of his clothes there along with some papers. The guy owning the place was just interested in his rent and didn't care about what he did. Brian stocked enough canned food for a month and plenty of reading material so that he could stay inside without having to come out in the event of things going wrong. This place really made him feel secure. He had his bolt hole.

One night Ernest invited him down to eat with him and his wife, and it soon became a ritual. Brian would take them out one night a week for dinner to repay their kindness. He was playing cards with them one night when he used a Yorkshire expression. He had done this a few times at first, but he explained it away by saying he worked in Yorkshire for a short time before coming to London and he did it purposely as a joke. It was accepted as such, but the incident made him more careful.

Visiting Annie and Bill presented problems—the disguise had to be removed—but he had difficulty shedding the accent. He practiced it so much that it was now second nature to use it, so he told them he was threatened and was altering things so he could cope. Annie worried, but she believed everything he told her and was soon satisfied.

Everyday that passed made him feel more secure. He felt he had covered everything but he had no way to know if The Organization would search for him. He decided when the time came, he had to break away with no half measures. He decided to gradually make changes in his appearance while keeping his regular routine with The Organization, then make the final break and assume his new identity, hoping they wouldn't find him before he left the country. This was not the first time he started a new life—only this time he felt his life was really on the line. Timing was everything.

For a number of months he had been a member of a golf club and was learning to play the game well. He enjoyed riding out to the club and the change of scenery—now he stopped going. Instead, he started to visit a working man's club and sat down to have a game of cards with the members. He had played cards in the army, so was a fair hand and could hold his own. The news of the neighbourhood was bandied around amongst the men, and he was soon a part of the grapevine. The men knew everything that went on but of course they did not know of The Organization. Eventually, he did hear of the strange disappearance of a young man from Crabb Court.

Brian set up charts in the apartment reminding him of things he had to do at different times and he had himself sign them at regular intervals. He was constantly checking and rechecking himself so as not to let his guard down.

During this time, he had the small cleft in his chin removed and his nose re-shaped. With good cooking he had put on about twenty pounds. He became used to the high lift shoes and never wore any other. Even his slippers were high-lifts, in the event that he walked out in the hall. He had a couple of scares, but they turned out to be nothing—just his over-wrought imagination. Still, he had not been lulled into a sense of false security and began to think that enough time had elapsed for him to make his final move.

He booked for a week at Brighton—a nice seaside town. There he had new photos taken for the latest passport—in the name he had been using. He was, for all intents and purposes, "Len Healey." And he was pretty sure he could be him for the rest of his life.

Sitting one night in the apartment after his holiday, he decided on one last test. As "Len Healey" he would visit Leeds and his old stomping grounds.

Taking the early bus, he traveled north to Manchester, where he changed buses and arrived in Leeds at midday. Then he booked a room near City Square at the Carlton Arms. It was a beautiful, warm spring day, which he took as a good omen. Taking a bus to the cemetery, he walked to his Mam and Dad's grave, stopping a long time to visit with them, and left a big bunch of flowers.

He walked around City Center and was amazed to see how things had changed and was disturbed to see some of the old places were gone. After a late dinner, he rode a Dewsbury Road bus out to The Tommy Wass Pub, where he had spent many a happy hour when on leave from the army. He knew his old football buddies would be there as loud as ever. The place was crowded even on a Tuesday night. Elbowing his way to the bar, and ordering pint of bitter ale, he stood alone. Nobody paid the slightest attention to him. After a few minutes, he saw the usual dart game going on at the rear, and one of the players was Donny Clay, the guy who had stolen his girl friend so long ago. Donny looked a little bit older, but otherwise was in good shape. Brian pushed his way over to the dart game. Standing on one side, he watched Clay take his shots and then Donny stood next to him. "Arratta," said Clay,"dos ta play darts?"

Brian replied, "Fine, yes thank you." It was wonderful to hear the Yorkshire dialect again. Clay was looking for free beer and spotted what he thought was a stranger (usually an easy mark). Brian introduced himself as "Len Healey" in his soft Belfast accent.

Brian played a couple of games and lost. It cost him three pounds for beer, but he stayed until closing time talking to these old buddies very carefully. There was never a mention of Brian Tilson, which was what he was alert for. He knew then his disguise was good. If these old friends couldn't spot him, no one else would be able to.

Looking around he thought in triumph, "I will never have to scratch around like this—I can buy this place, lock, stock and barrel." Then he wondered sadly, was it worth it?

Chapter 40

Brian returned to London in very high spirits. He felt he could move anywhere he wanted to now and his secrets were safe. He also decided that from now on he was going to make amends for some of the wrongs he had done—although he was sure that he had also done a lot of good—ridding the world of some people who, in his opinion, deserved to die.

Brian immediately submitted papers to emigrate to the United States. This was a long, tedious task, as he had to be very careful with the forged papers, but everything went smoothly, allowing his final plan to take shape.

He was really surprised by how generous The Organization had been with its payments. At last count he had taken care of thirty six clients. With all his payouts, he still had a sum of 220,000 pounds cash in the bank, enough to start a new life overseas—he need never worry about income again. He made arrangements that if he had not made contact with the bank for sixty days, his sister Annie would be notified. His safety box would be opened. All the papers explaining his financial dealings would be there in detail.

She could then investigate to see if he were still alive. He felt that should take care of almost everything.

After three months, Brian was notified that his application had been OK'd. He began to sell all his belongings. He had rid himself of anything that tied him to Brian Tilson, and The Organization. Now he double-checked everything. He never felt better than when he booked a flight to New York for three weeks hence.

Riding down the Showcross to visit Annie and Bill before he left, he was extra careful. He didn't want any slip-ups at this late stage. Despite his hard shell, he loved Annie and her family. But when he looked at Annie, Bill and the two children, he felt a strong wave of revulsion against himself. He was sickened at what he had become and how he had allowed avarice and ambition to corrupt and ruin his life. This would be better for all of them—for him to disappear. He couldn't say good-bye fast enough. He couldn't go on forever looking over his shoulder, and having the fear of again being discovered by The Organization. He had served them for more than four years and wanted no more. He fully intended this to be the last time he would see his folks. Now he would sever his ties completely, hoping he had not endangered them by his connections.

Returning to London after his visit, he re-checked the papers. He had just made himself a big pint pot of tea (like all Yorkshire men he loved his tea and he never had been able to break himself of his big pint pot). As he walked to the chair, the phone rang, startling him. He was so startled he placed his full-to-the-brim pot down, spilling some tea. It was Ernie (his landlord) asking him to come down to see him the next morning.

When he picked up the pot, he found that the tea had spoiled some of the forged immigration papers. Upon further close examination, he realized that they would not pass in their present state. He cursed himself for his stupidity—now he would have to return to Mr. Moore to get them renewed.

As darkness fell he visited Mr. Moore and placed his problem in front of him. Moore said, "Two 'ours and two 'undred pounds" So Brian sat to wait. As the job was completed, he handed the cash over and then Mr. Moore froze him—"For another two 'undred pounds ah am going to do ya t'biggest favour ya have ever 'ad done." He looked directly at Brian and held out his hand. Brian didn't hesitate, but handed over the two hundred pounds.

"Two of Morrell's men were round 'ere a few weeks since axing about ya." (Morrell was a big time owner of a night club in the Elephant and Castle area and Brian had already met him.) "They 'ad a very poor picture of ya. Ah told 'em nutting, but ah must tell 'em ya 'ave been 'ere na, and give 'em ya'r address. Somebody may 'ave seen ya come 'ere, and ah can't risk it. Ya know what would 'appear t'me, if ah didn't. Ya can belt me one in t'chops and ah'll be an 'our afore ah turn ya in. Son, ya'r in deep trouble."

Old Moore looked at him with sincere compassion as he told him all this and then shook his head. Brian looked at the old man and the thought entered his head, "One dart will cover my tracks here." Instead, he **did** belt the old man and took off as fast as he could for his apartment. He had almost everything ready, so he threw his papers and a few things in a small suitcase. As he began to unscrew the window, he heard loud voices downstairs.

Quietly opening the door, he heard Joe Batten, one of Morrell's thugs saying, "We'll 'ave a look for ourselves." Brian quickly locked the door and rammed a leather slipper under the edge, jamming it, as he heard footsteps on the stairs.

He put out all the lights, opened the rear window and quickly dropped down onto the shop roof. There he stopped and looked down onto the street below. He was taking no chance of anyone being down there waiting for him. His heart was in his mouth. It was now or never! The street looked OK—and there was still no sign of pursuit—the slipper must have delayed them.

As he slipped down the pipe, his knees caught on the fastening, half-way down. He felt his pants tear and the warm blood flow from a rip in his knee. The pain was excruciating. As he reached the pavement, he bent down to tie his handkerchief on the leg to staunch the flow of blood.

Then he saw two big men coming slowly toward him. "Daft bugger," said one as they passed.

He ducked into the darkness and hobbled away as fast as he could on a circuitous route to his other apartment on Hill Street.

Brian stayed in the apartment for a full week, waiting for his sore knee to heal. He had gone without shaving to give his beard time to grow, and he was feeling the effects of not having any fresh food or air. His sleep had been really bad. Finally he went to a phone and called Ernie back.

"Ernie, this is Len. How are you doing? Can we talk?" he asked.

"Len, it's good ta 'ear ya'r," said Ernie in a tight voice. "Where are ya? And where 'ave ya been? Two fellers came lucking for ya, right after ya came in that night. They said ya owned money for a gambling debt and they had come to collect. They forced me ta let 'em into your apartment—and they tuk everything out of there. Me and Sylvia thought it better to not interfere. One of t'em stayed out front—in fact, I think he is still there, waiting for ya to come back. We've been worried about ya."

"OK, Ernie, I'll be all right. Now don't you worry about anything— I'll write you later and fill you in. Good-bye for now." And he rung off.

He returned to the Hill Street apartment, this time with some fresh supplies. He checked his papers. He was sure no one knew of his flight plans—so he continued to stay put.

He had plenty of time now to think things out, and he realized that after all this time he still didn't know how many people were in The Organization. He had met such a very few, and this was his main worry. He realized now that from the start, he should have been trying to get to know who was who, in order to safe-guard himself later, but he had been complacent and allowed things to slide. He had not covered his own back. Now there was no way but to luck it out. He felt he had done everything possible he could do.

It was still dark on the morning of his flight—it was leaving very early. He walked to the end of the street, caught a cab and went all the way to Heathrow Airport, carrying one small briefcase, arriving just before flight time. He had trimmed his beard to a small, neat goatee, and with his best worsted suit he looked spick and span—although tired, drawn and much older. No different from the dozens of business men traveling that day.

As he walked to the boarding ramp, his knee was still bothering him and he walked slowly and stiffly. His heart was pounding, and he had a hard time stopping himself from looking around, but he kept a tight grip on himself. A red dart in a cigarette packet in his top pocket was at the ready. He realized that now everything depended on the next fifteen minutes. He picked up a copy of the morning paper so he could cover his face as he waited in the passenger lounge.

After boarding, he settled in his seat, his knotted stomach relaxed slowly as he permitted himself a look around. He could see no cause of alarm. As the 747 jet zoomed aloft, headed for New York, he finally slept, exhausted.

About the Author

Henry J. Howley is a man of many talents, who has woven the rich detail of his life experiences into his writing.

He was born at Batley, a small historical town mentioned in the 1086 Doomsday Survey of William the Conqueror. Batley lies between Leeds, Wakefield, Huddersfield and Bradford in Yorkshire, England. The Yorkshire dialect and lifestyle is vividly portrayed in his book along with his picture of other areas of the British Isles.

His father served for four and a half years in the British Army and was gassed in World War I. The family emigrated to the United States in December 1919, but tragically, Henry's father died the day they reached their new homeland. It was the day after Christmas, known as Boxing Day. Henry's mother returned to England with her seven children (one unborn) and supported them by working in a rag warehouse.

His brother Michael went to work in the coal mines at fourteen and grew up to be the middleweight wrestling champion of the British Isles. Michael later served in the army along with two other brothers and a sister. Henry finished school at fourteen, after winning a gold medal for swimming. He worked as a mechanic and bricklayer, then signed forms to become a professional footballer. He won a silver cup for amateur rugby, but turned to professional wrestling for fourteen years.

Henry broke his shoulder two days before World War II, making him ineligible to serve as a soldier. So he used his talents singing and wrestling to entertain the troops in army camps throughout the British Isles.

In 1943 he married his wife, Sylvia, who was serving in the Womens Auxiliary Air Force. In November 1949, along with their son David (who later served in the 8th Army Airforce), the Howleys emigrated to America where their daughter Susan was born. Henry wrestled in the United States and retired after a very successful wrestling trip to Mexico.

Under the Official Secrets Act, he worked as a building erection supervisor in Pentagon defense plants throughout the United States and Canada. He sat for his final examination for Chief Construction Code Certificate. His "crowning glory," however, was to make the Dean's List at Gloucester County College in New Jersey.

After an early retirement due to an accident, Henry and Sylvia moved to Florida where he attended classes in writing and spends his time writing novels about the assassins trained by violent professions of the world. **The Making of An Assassin** is the first in a series of three novels.

Henry writes short stories and poetry and enjoys singing tenor in a number of choirs, including the Venice Cathedral.